Changing Babies
and other stories

DEBORAH MOGGACH

Changing Babies
and other stories

HEINEMANN : LONDON

First published in Great Britain 1995
by William Heinemann Ltd
an imprint of Reed Consumer Books Ltd
Michelin House, 81 Fulham Road, London SW3 6RB
and Auckland, Melbourne, Singapore and Toronto

A CIP catalogue record for this title
is available from the British Library

ISBN 0 434 00243 7

Phototypeset by Intype, London
Printed and bound in Great Britain
by Mackays of Chatham plc

For Csaba

These stories, sometimes slightly amended, were first published
or broadcast in the following:

Changing Babies – first broadcast on Radio 4, then printed
in *Telling Stories* and *Best Short Stories 1991*

Suspicion – first broadcast on Radio 4, then printed in
Good Housekeeping and *Telling Stories 3*

Ta for the Memories – published in *The Daily Telegraph*

Stopping at the Lights – published in *New Writing 2*

How I Learnt to be a Real Countrywoman – first published in *The Times*,
then broadcast on Radio 4 and published in *Telling Stories 1*

Family Feelings – Five Linked Stories – first broadcast on Radio 4

A Pedicure in Florence – published in *Freedom* (Red Cross anthology)

Summer Bedding – published in *Marie Claire*

Lucky Dip – published in *She*

Empire Building – first published in *Fiction Magazine*, and then in *Smile*

Stiff Competition – first appeared in *Cosmopolitan*, and then in *Smile*

Buzz – An Eighties Soap Opera in Five Parts – published in *Cosmopolitan*

Contents

Changing Babies

Duncan was only little, but he noticed more than they thought. He knew, for instance, when the phone rang and it was his Dad on the other end, because his mother always got out her cigarettes. She only smoked when his Dad phoned up.

He knew Christmas was coming, but everybody knew that. In the shops, tinsel was strewn over microwave cookers. There was a crib at school, with a black baby in it. He had already opened two doors in his advent calendar. Inside the first door was a bike and inside the second was a walkman. 'My God!' chortled his mother. 'It'll be video recorders next! The Bethlehem Shopping Experience! No baby Jesus at the end, just a credit card hotline!'

No Jesus! There had to be a baby; it was Christmas. He wanted to open the last door, just to make sure, but he didn't dare.

It was his Granny who told him the Christmas story. She said that the birth of Jesus was a miracle, and that Joseph wasn't his real father. God was. Sometimes she took Duncan to church. She went up to the altar to eat God's body. Once, when they came home for lunch, she tried to make him do it too. 'Come on,' she said. 'Eat it up, it's good for you. Look, *I'm* eating it. Mmmmm ... lovely cod.'

Apart from that moment of alarm he liked being with his Granny. She watched TV with him, sitting on the sofa; she wasn't always doing something else. She kept photos of him in a proper book, with dates under his name, instead of all muddled loose in a drawer. She smelt of powder. She wasn't always talking on the phone. Nowadays she came to his house a lot, to babysit. Before he went to bed, she made him say his prayers. When she wasn't there he whispered them, so his Mum couldn't hear.

His Mum didn't pray; she did exercises. Once he went into her bedroom and she was kneeling down. He thought she was praying for his Dad to come home but she said she was tightening her stomach muscles. He often got things wrong; there were so many big, tiring adjustments he had to make. Anyway, she didn't want his Dad back. She was always on the phone to her friends. 'He never thought of *my* needs' she said. 'He's so cut off from his feelings, so bloody self-absorbed. He didn't notice how I was growing, he's just like a child! It would take a miracle to change him.' But Christmas was a time of miracles, wasn't it? That was the point.

His Dad had moved into a flat with a metal thing on the door which his voice squawked through. His mother would stand there in the street, shouting at its little slits. His Dad's voice sounded like a Dalek's; 'What?' he said. 'What?' He could never hear what she was saying. She never came in. The hall smelt of school dinners. The flat smelt of new paint.

Duncan visited his Dad twice a week. He slept on the sofa. Its cushion had a silky fringe which he sucked before he went to sleep. His Dad talked on the phone a lot, too. When he had finished he would take him out. If it was raining they went to the swimming baths. If it wasn't raining they went to the Zoo. Duncan knew every corner of the Zoo, even the places hardly anyone went, like the cages where boring brown birds stayed hidden. At school Duncan impressed his teacher, he could recite the names of so many unusual animals. Years later, when he was a grown man, words like 'tapir' and 'aardvark' always made him sad.

Christmas was getting nearer. He had opened seven doors on his advent calendar now. He went shopping with his Dad and they bought a very small Christmas tree. They walked past office buildings. Old men sat in the doorways, their heads poking out of cardboard boxes. 'Huh. They've been thrown out too,' said his Dad. Motorbikes leant against the pavement, chattering to themselves. But Duncan kept quiet. He wanted to ask his Dad if he was coming back for Christmas but he didn't dare. Instead he searched the pavement for rubber bands the postman had dropped.

They stood at the bus stop. When he was with his Dad they were always waiting for things. For a waitress to come, when they sat in a café. For the bus, because his Dad didn't have the car.

'At school,' Duncan said, 'we've got a black baby Jesus.'

'Very p.c.' laughed his Dad, whatever that meant. Pee-see?

'Last Christmas there was a pink one.' He was suddenly conscious of the stretch of time, since a year had passed, and how old he was to remember. What had happened to the pink baby? It couldn't have grown older like he had, it couldn't have learnt to walk; it was just pretend. Had they thrown it away? But it was supposed to be Jesus.

His Dad rubbed Duncan's hands. 'Bloody buses,' he said. 'Where's your gloves?'

'I took them out.' They had been threaded through his coat-sleeves, on elastic. 'I'm not a *baby*,' he said.

The bus came at last. They got out at the late-night supermarket. It was called Payless but his Dad called it Paymore. They bought some Jaffa cakes. Back in the flat the phone was ringing. It wasn't his mother; his Dad didn't turn his back and lower his voice. He spoke quite normally.

' . . . they've had to re-edit the whole damn thing,' he

5

said. 'Nobody told them at Channel Four. It'll take another four weeks. Frank's incensed.'

Frankincense! The word billowed out, magically.

His father was still talking. ' . . . I'd better bring it round myself,' he said, 'by hand . . .'

Duncan had sucked the chocolate off his Jaffa cake. He dozed on the sofa. To tell the truth it was way past his bedtime, but he wasn't saying anything. He closed his eyes. His father, wearing a flowing robe, knocked on the door on Christmas Day. He would come and visit, carrying gold and frankincense and the other thing. He would come.

Duncan pressed his face into the cushion. He felt his father gently pulling the collection of rubber bands off his wrist.

The next morning he was back home. He opened the eighth door on his advent calendar. A doll – ugh! After lunch his mother took him swimming. She had threaded the gloves back through his coat-sleeves but he refused to put them on; they flopped at his wrists. 'Next stop, hooliganism!' she said, whatever that meant. 'Glue-sniffing. Truancy. It's all my fault!'

At the pool they had another struggle with his water wings. He said he was too old for them now. She liked him wearing them because it meant he could bob around in the water while she swam to the deep bit, up and down for miles. She said she had to do a unit of exercise a day, which meant twenty minutes. She told somebody on the phone that it was part of her *Cosmopolitan* Shape-Up Plan. 'I'm going to take pride in my body,' she said. 'It's had years of neglect. It's like one of those old churches nobody's been into for years.' She had laughed loudly at this, but he didn't see why it was funny.

He bobbed up and down in the water. A sticking plaster floated nearby. He liked collecting sticking plasters and lining them up on the edge of the pool. In fact he loved everything about the pool. When he came with his parents they used to laugh together and splash each other. They mucked around like children, and the black stuff from his mother's eyes ran down her cheeks. There was a shallow, baby's bit and an elephant slide. In the deeper bit a whistle blew and the waves started, which was thrilling. He liked wearing the rubber band with the locker key on it, this made him feel important. There was a machine where you could buy crisps; the bag swung like a monkey along the bar and dropped into the chute. He loved going there. That was why it was so terrible, what happened.

After his mother had swum her unit they got out. She wrapped him in a towel and he watched her as she stood under the shower, rubbing her head with shampoo. She sang, much too loudly: *'I'm going to wash that man right out of my hair!'* She didn't mind people seeing her bare, either; she was always striding around the changing rooms, wobble-wobble. His Dad did too; everything swinging about. When his parents were together, and they all came to the swimming pool, Duncan would run from the men's cubicles to the ladies' ones, depending on which parent was being the least embarrassing. But nowadays he had to stay in one place.

Anyway, this particular day he had got dressed. His mother was drying her hair. In the corner of the changing room he saw something he hadn't seen before: it was a big red plastic thing, on legs, like a crib. He nudged his Mum and pointed.

'What's that for?' he shouted.

She switched off the dryer. 'What's what for?'

'That.' He pointed.

'Oh, it's for changing babies,' she said, and she switched on the dryer again.

That night his Mum went out and his Granny came to

babysit. She tut-tutted around the house, as usual. She opened the fridge and wrinkled her nose.

'Jiff and a J-cloth,' she said, 'that's all it needs. But they're all too busy nowadays, aren't they? Lord, this yoghurt's covered with mould!' She put all his Mum's empty wine bottles in plastic bags and dumped them outside the front door. 'Hope *she* didn't drink all these,' she muttered. Then she sat with him while he ate his supper.

'You've been very quiet,' she said. 'I know what you're thinking about! All the things you'd like for Christmas!'

He didn't reply.

'Come on, poppet,' she said. 'Aren't you going to eat up your lovely fish fingers?'

Later she washed up. Usually the clatter comforted him; Granny putting things in order. Tonight it didn't work. He was thinking about the red plastic crib. Which babies did it change? Any baby that climbed into it? If his mother put him there, what would happen? At school they had taken away the old baby and put in another one. His mother was always changing things. Granny's presents, for instance. Granny gave her clothes and she took them back to Harvey Nichols. 'Eek! What does she want me to look like – Judith Chalmers?' She would come home with something completely different. And only last week she had stared angrily at her bed, as if she had never looked at it before. 'Paisley's so *seventies*!' she had said. She had yanked off the duvet cover and squashed it into a rubbish bag. 'Memories, memories.'

His head spun. When Granny was getting him ready for bed he said: 'Tell me about Jesus in the manger again.'

'I'd read it to you if only I could find a Bible,' she said. She looked through the bookshelves, clicking her tongue. '*The Female Underclass*,' she said. '*Aggression and Gender*. No Bible, honestly! My own daughter!'

Undressing him, she told him the story. He squeezed

his eyes shut. 'Virgin Mary . . .' he heard. ' . . . wrapped him in swaddling clothes and laid him in a manger . . .'

She took him into the bathroom to brush his teeth. He suddenly saw the carrier bag, from swimming. It sat slumped in the corner, bulging with his damp towel and swimming trunks; the washing machine was broken. The bag had big letters on it: VIRGIN MEGASTORE. He stared at it, hypnotized.

Swaddling clothes . . . Virgin Mary . . . He tried to work it out but it was all so difficult. He was in bed now, his eyes shut. What was wrapped up in swaddling clothes, lying in the Virgin bag? Did he ever dare unwrap it?

His Granny kissed him goodnight. 'Their behaviour beats me,' she murmured. 'Honestly, why don't they grow up?'

'I am growing up,' he said, sleepily.

She laid her cheek against his; he smelt her powder. 'Poor little thing,' she sighed.

In the morning he didn't open the next door in his advent calendar. He didn't want to get to the end. There was something terrible inside the last door, just as there was something terrible inside the Virgin bag.

Granny rang up while he was watching TV. He was watching his video of 'The Magic Roundabout', even though he knew it was babyish. Babyish things made him feel safe.

He heard his mother talking to Granny. ' . . . honestly, Ma, the dustmen have just taken away all the bottles I was going to recycle, two months' worth! Haven't you any morals? What's going to happen to the planet?' Her voice lowered. ' . . . I know, but I wish you wouldn't interfere. Not in that, either. He's perfectly all right. I'm the one who looks after him all the time, I should know. He's just lost his appetite . . . I know it's all very difficult, you needn't tell *me*, but it's not all my fault, do you know what Alan did last week – '

Duncan climbed to his feet and turned up the sound of 'The Magic Roundabout', very loud.

His mother tried to make him go swimming on Tuesday, after school, but he refused to go. He knew exactly what she was planning. She was going to wrap him up in a towel and put him into the crib. Jesus had no father, just like him. Granny said: 'We're all children of God.'

He heard his mother on the phone, talking to one of her friends. 'I know why Duncan doesn't want to go swimming,' she whispered. 'It's because his father goes and we sometimes see him there. These bloody freelances, never know where they'll pop up. When he sees his father unexpectedly he gets really upset.'

It was odd. She never called him 'Dad' anymore. She called him 'his father'. It made his Dad sound awesome, like somebody in the Lord's Prayer. *Our Father, which art in heaven* . . .

She had got it all wrong, of course, about swimming. Grown-ups got everything wrong. But he couldn't possibly tell her. He started crying, so she took him out to buy a Christmas tree instead. It was much bigger than Dad's. They decorated it with tinsel and bags of chocolate money that made the branches droop, but when she switched on the lights they didn't work. She shouted a rude word. Then she muttered: 'First the washing machine, then the guttering, now the bloody lights. Christ, I need a man!' She looked as if she was about to cry, too. She went to the phone and dialled a number. 'Is Mr Weisman home yet?' she asked. 'I've been phoning him for two days!'

Duncan stopped peeling a chocolate coin. He sat bolt upright. Mr Wise Man?

It was all getting more and more confusing. The next day

his Dad collected him from school and took him back to his flat. He had put the very small Christmas tree into a flowerpot.

Duncan sat in front of the TV. There wasn't a lot to do in his Dad's flat. His Dad had bought a box of Snakes and Ladders but they had lost the dice. He pushed his jeep around the carpet for a bit, making noises to encourage himself, but then he stopped. He thought about the Wise Man. He mustn't come! If he came, Christmas would start and it would all be wrong! It was already going horribly wrong. He had to do something about it.

Dad was in the kitchen part of the room, frying sausages. His jacket lay over a chair. Duncan put his hand in the pocket and pulled out his Dad's wallet. He wanted to see if his photo was still inside.

There he was. And there was the photo of his mother, holding him when he was a baby. She was smiling. But he wasn't reassured. The room grew smokier. 'Baked beans, or baked beans?' called out his Dad.

He pulled out his Dad's Access card, and his video club card. Then he pulled out another one. It said: *I would like to help someone live after my death*. He turned the card over. *Kidneys*, it said on the back, *Eyes Heart Pancreas Liver*, it said. *I request, that after my death, any part of my body be used for the treatment of others*.

On Thursday Mr Wise Man still hadn't come. His mother cried: 'My life's going to pieces!'

So was his. When the Wise Man came, he was going to take somebody away. Jesus died on the cross, said Granny, so that the rest of us could live. That's what his Dad was going to do; that's why he had the card in his wallet. And then everybody ate him because he was God.

'Why don't you want to go swimming?' asked his mother. 'You used to love it.'

That night he heard her on the phone. 'We've got to

11

settle this, Alan.' Even upstairs, he could smell her cigarette smoke. 'You keep putting it off. What are we going to do about Christmas? Are you going to have him, or me?'

Duncan pulled the duvet over his head. They were going to saw him in half, like a leg of lamb.

The next morning the phone rang. His mother was in the lavatory so he answered it. A voice said: 'Mr Weisman here, chief. Can I speak to your good mother?'

'No!' he shouted, and put the receiver back.

But the Wise Man was going to come. It was Duncan's last day at school and his Granny fetched him home. When they opened the door his Mum said: 'Thank God Mr Weisman's coming. He'll be here at six.'

Duncan thought, fast. Then he had an idea. He pulled at his mother's leg. 'I want to go swimming!' he said urgently. 'Let's go!'

And it worked. His mother smiled. 'Darling, I'm so glad!' she said.

Granny said: 'I'll stay here and let Mr Weisman in.'

While they were talking Duncan ran upstairs and dialled his Dad's number. He needed to see him, badly. But only the answerphone answered, his Dad's voice all stiff and formal, so he left a message. 'Come to the swimming pool. Please!'

In the changing room he scuttled past the crib, fast. And then he was in the water, with his mother. There wasn't pop music today; they were playing *Rudolph the Red-Nosed Reindeer*. He was bobbing around when the whistle blew and the waves started, tossing him up and down, and suddenly his father was there, his arms outstretched. His parents were shouting at each other but Duncan couldn't hear, there were so many other people in the pool, their voices echoing. They squealed when the waves came, rocking the water and splashing over the sides. Duncan was tossed towards his father, who held him; then he was tossed back to his mother, who pulled him to her. The black stuff was running down her face. Spluttering, he was grabbed by strong arms, then the waves pulled him away.

He was in the changing room now, and his mother was rubbing him dry. She did it so hard it hurt. His Dad's voice shouted, from the men's cubicles. 'You can't live without me, Victoria! You know that!'

'Shut up!' she shouted. 'I'm managing perfectly well!'

'You're such a liar!' he shouted. 'I know you inside out!'

'You've never known me! You're too bloody selfish!'

'Me? Selfish?' He bellowed with laughter.

'It takes one to know one!' she shouted.

'I love you!' he shouted.

Duncan cowered; everybody was listening. This was worse than them being bare.

'Look at what it's doing to Duncan!' shouted his Dad. 'He doesn't understand. He thinks it's all his fault, he's getting terribly disturbed. He's started wetting the bed again!'

Duncan froze. How *could* his Dad say that? He darted out of the cubicle, into the open part. There was a baby lying in the crib; its mother was changing its nappy. He dashed for the exit, but just then his Dad appeared, nearly naked. He grabbed Duncan and held him tightly.

Duncan pressed his face against him; he smelt of chlorine.

When they got home Mr Weisman had been. The lights sparkled on the Christmas tree. The washing machine worked; his mother bundled the damp towels into it. She was panting; she seemed out of breath. Later, after supper, she put on her red woolly dress and squirted perfume on her neck. She kept telling Duncan to go to bed, but in a vague way as if she was looking for something.

Later that night his Dad came home. Duncan heard his suitcase bumping against the banisters as he came upstairs. Light slid into Duncan's room when he opened the door, just a bit. He stood there for a moment but he didn't come in. The next morning his stripy spongebag was back in the bidet and his computer was back on his desk. On Christmas Eve he helped Duncan open the last door on his advent calendar, and there was the baby Jesus. He had been there all the time.

In fact, his Dad didn't just stay for Christmas. He stayed at home for good. When Duncan was older, he sometimes thought of his father's six-month absence, and the way it had ended. And he told himself: the swimming pool wasn't just for changing babies. Not as it turned out. It was for changing grown-ups, too.

Suspicion

He seemed such a normal bloke. That's how they get away with it I suppose, looking normal. He looked like a real football-playing, I'm-in-sales, make-mine-a-double-scotch sort of bloke. That's what attracted me in the first place. After the waifs and strays I'd been out with he seemed so male. I mean, he actually looked as if he could drive a car.

His name was Kenneth McTurk and I met him when he came in for a glass of guava juice. He'd just been to the acupuncturist upstairs – the café where I work, it's in this building full of ists, reflexologists, aromatherapists, all that alternative stuff that's not so alternative anymore since Prince Charles took it up.

He sat at the counter, rubbing his back. 'By Jesus, I feel like a pin-cushion,' he said. 'You seen the size of those needles?'

He had an Irish accent – beguiling, almost female in such a beefy man. He had a ruddy face and sticking-out ears; they gave him a boyish look. He wore a suit – *nobody* wore a suit in our place. He was one of those fidgety men who are always jangling their car keys. He said that he was a martyr to his back, stress-related said his doctor, and why not give acupuncture a whirl? So he had looked it up in the yellow pages.

'A load of mumbo-jumbo, my love, if you're asking my opinion,' he said. 'Now would you recommend the carrot cake?' I said it was made with bran. 'I see I've entered a bowel-friendly environment,' he replied. 'I suppose a cheroot is out of the question?'

17

It was, but the place was empty. So he had a smoke and we introduced ourselves.

'Velda,' he said. 'Now that's unusual.'

'It means wise woman,' I said, and laughed. When it came to men, never had anybody been so ludicrously misnamed.

The next day, when I was cashing up, he walked in and said he was taking me out for a drink. Well, why not? He made me feel flushed and reckless. As we walked towards his car he stopped at the NatWest, plucked a sprig of fuschia from its windowbox, and put it in my hair. When we arrived at his car he blithely removed a 'Doctor on Emergency Call' sticker from the windscreen.

'I know you're not a doctor,' I said. 'What *do* you do?'

'Bit of this, bit of that.' He tapped the side of his nose with his finger. 'Import export.'

Until then I had only seen dodgy men in TV series. I suppose I lived a sheltered existence, me and my cats and the long-running non-event of my love-life. Suddenly here I was, sitting in a flash car with an unknown middle-aged man who jumped the lights and filled the air with cheroot smoke. He said the acupuncturist had been a con-artist and I said boldly: 'Takes one to know one.'

He laughed and told me about a practical joke he had played on somebody, a bloke he'd once worked with. He had filled the drawers of the chap's desk with water and put some goldfish in them. Did I believe him? Who cares. It was so insanely silly that I fell in love with him, then and there.

He took me to a pub in Kilburn. It was big and noisy. Two fiddlers played, they were called the McDougal Brothers, and I drank a pint of Guinness – me, Velda, who was usually in bed by ten with a cup of herbal tea. There was a raffle for a fluffy elephant and I didn't want to join in because it was so hideous but Kenneth insisted. 'Fund-raising,' he said.

'Funds for what?'

But he just put his finger on the side of his nose. I hadn't a clue what he was talking about but by then everything was getting swimmy and suddenly there was this furry thing in my arms – not Kenny but the elephant, I had won it – and I was in his car and next thing we were sitting in a restaurant drinking champagne and the next thing I remember it was Kenneth in my arms and my duvet over us and the sound of my cats scratching at the kitchen door where I had shut them away.

A couple of weeks later he moved in. Not that he brought much with him – just a suitcase of clothes. But there he was, a full-grown man, knocking into the furniture and whistling in my bathroom – he even managed to whistle while he shaved, *My Way* with a buzzing accompaniment. I bought him Ty-Phoo teabags and – proof of my love – bacon for breakfast. I'm a vegetarian, you see. With him in it, six-foot-two, my flat looked stuffy and spinsterly, with its batik hangings and its bowls of pot-pourri, but he said it was so peaceful. He said it was like stepping into another world, a Bedouin tent with just me and him.

'It's a battlefield out there, Velda my love,' he said, lying on the bed with his arms around the elephant. A joss-stick spiralled smoke one side and a cheroot spiralled smoke on the other. 'You've no idea of it.'

He charmed me. He even charmed Mrs Prichard upstairs, carrying her shopping and flirting with her, though she's eighty-three. He made me feel as if I was the most bewitching woman in the world, my skin blushed, I bloomed for him. He told me I was beautiful, voluptuous, a goddess. He wrote lewd suggestions in the steam on the bathroom mirror. And flowers, oh the flowers! When he arrived late, the nodding heads of them wrapped in fancy paper from the all-night shop in Westbourne Grove.

He often arrived late and left early. Or he would be home for the afternoon and leave after supper. He never got any phone calls and I never met any of his friends but I didn't mind, he and I were cocooned in ourselves, we had no need of anything. My job at the café was part-time so I fitted in with him. As for his job – well, he was very mysterious about it. He only said it involved a lot of travel and in fact he was away a great deal, days on end sometimes. I wasn't suspicious. Believe it or not, I wasn't even suspicious when I found the handcuffs. Or not for the right reason.

It happened like this. Kenny had been living with me for two weeks and we had just come home from the pictures. I realized I had left my shawl in his car so I found his jacket, which was hanging up in the hallway, and fished for his car keys. In the pocket I felt something heavy, wrapped in a paper bag. I took it out. Just at that moment he came out of the kitchen. I held out the pair of handcuffs and laughed.

'Oh-oh, bondage-time!'

His face reddened. Then he recovered himself and laughed. 'Tie me up!' He shoved a cloth in my hand. 'Here, the killer tea towel! Whip me to a frenzy! I like it, I like it!'

Another odd thing happened that evening. He said he was just popping out for some cheroots. I watched him from the window. Why? I don't know. He crossed the street and walked towards Westbourne Grove. But he stopped at the phone box on the corner, looked around, and went in. I watched him – a small, solitary figure in the illuminated booth. Somebody familiar always shrinks, don't they, when they think they are unobserved. Why was he making a secret phone call? In my area of Bayswater the phone booths are plastered with hookers' cards – *I'm Lorraine,*

Spank Me! Strict French Lessons! I remember thinking: suppose he *is* a bondage-freak. That's why he's always popping out. He's ringing up one of them now. Lorraine or someone.

I didn't say anything. He was away too much for me to spoil our short times together by wife-type accusations. The next morning, however, he seemed edgy and abstracted. When I went into the bedroom, after breakfast, he was shoving a pair of muddy trainers into a carrier bag. When he saw me he stopped, dropped the bag behind the bed and put his arms around me.

'I have to go away for a couple of days,' he said. 'Oh Velda my lovely, if you knew how much I wished it was you and me alone in the world, far away from all this.'

'From all what?'

'It's dangerous out there, see. A man, he's weak. Maybe he's young and foolish. He makes a mistake maybe once in his life and then he's caught like a fly in a spider's web. They have him there, where they want him. He can run, but he can't hide. He can hide, but he can't run.'

He kissed the tip of my nose and then he was gone, carrier bag and all.

That night there was an explosion in the Territorial Army Barracks in Albany Street, near Regent's Park. Four men were injured – it was a miracle it wasn't more – but half the place was gutted. The IRA claimed responsibility and issued a statement saying it was stepping up its mainland terrorist campaign.

I don't read the newspapers. I'm not a political sort of person. I saw it by chance on the front page of a *Guardian* that somebody had left in the café. Nothing clicked together, not even then. Nothing clicked until the following Thursday.

Kenneth had been back for a couple of days. Was it my imagination or was he changing? He looked fleshier – he was putting on weight. Maybe it was my lentil lasagne. And he snapped at Flapjack, my Burmese, when she was only playing with his shoe-laces.

It was early evening and I had to nip out to the shops. Halfway down the street, however, I realized I had forgotten my purse so I went back and let myself into the flat. Kenny was in the bedroom, speaking on the phone. I paused in the hallway.

'Let me speak to Fergus,' he said in a low voice. There was a pause, then he said: 'Fergus, you keep away from that gun, see? Any messing around and I'll be informing the boss. And you know what'll happen to you then, don't you?'

I let myself out of the flat and crept downstairs. I managed to make it to the end of the street and leaned against some railings. My heart hammered against my ribs. How could I have been so stupid? The shock was so great that when I tried to pull the facts together I had to haul them, slowly, as if I were drugged.

The handcuffs. The Republican pub in Kilburn. The terrorist explosion . . . The long, unexplained absences . . . The phone box and now the threatening telephone call . . .

Funnily enough, I wasn't alarmed, not for myself. In fact I felt a shameful tingle of excitement. This man I loved was suddenly strange to me. It didn't cross my mind, not yet, that he might be dangerous – that he might, in fact, be a killer. The whole thing seemed as disconnected and unlikely as some TV drama I happened to have stepped into, the sort of TV drama I never watched anyway, that was happening to someone else.

I was in the late-night supermarket, standing in front of a pork chop. A kidney nestled in the pallid flesh. I thought: I came out to buy some dinner and now a different Kenneth will be eating it. To someone like me a meat counter smells of death; it lurks there, inert, under the cellophane. I knew I mustn't think like this – I mustn't even *start* to think about killing or I wouldn't be able to behave normally when I got home. What was I supposed to be buying anyway? My mind was a blank. Beside me a rastafarian dipped up and down to the beat of his walkman; a woman shouldered me aside and pulled out a pack of sausages. Trolleys rattled and a tannoy boomed but it came from a thousand miles away. I had to get through this evening somehow, walk it through like a robot, until tomorrow came, Kenneth left for work and I could start to think clearly.

I went back home and let myself into the flat.

'Light of my life!' He pounced at me from behind and pinioned me against the wall. 'Five minutes you've gone, and it's an eternity!' His breath was hot on my face.

It had been an eternity. I had stepped out of one life and into another. Nothing would be the same, ever again.

It rained in the night. The next morning dawned shiny and innocent, the streets washed clean. I kissed Kenneth goodbye. The puddles winked at me. In the block of flats opposite someone opened a window, flashing a message to me. Or to him? Where was he going?

'Where are you going?' I asked.

'Liverpool' he said, quick as anything. 'A shipment's coming in.'

From Ireland? I couldn't bear to ask him. By questioning him, I felt it was me who was doing the betraying, not him. Ridiculous, I know.

His hair was slicked back, dark and wet, from the shower. His signet ring caught the sun as he scratched the side of his nose. I put my arms around him and held him tightly; silently I said goodbye to the old Kenneth. I smelt his familiar scent of tobacco and Aramis.

'There there,' he murmured, 'I'll be seeing you tomorrow.' He disentangled himself, glanced up and down the road and loaded his suitcase into the boot. I tried to help him but he wouldn't let me and slammed the boot shut. He was slightly breathless.

He drove off and I went inside, slowly. I felt very old. Mrs Prichard, hurrying downstairs, looked as spry as a girl.

'Is he gone, that naughty boy?' she asked, waving the *Daily Express*. 'I was going to tell him his stars.'

That's the only bit *I* used to read, I wanted to reply. The horoscopes. Now I understand why I never looked at the other pages.

'He likes to know it before he flies,' she said. 'These airline pilots are very superstitious.'

Oh Lord, he had lied to her, too.

I closed my front door. My cats pressed themselves against my legs. They pressed against his legs too, they didn't know the difference. I tried to practise my postural meditation but for once I couldn't concentrate. Squatting on the carpet, I stared at myself in the mirror: cloudy black hair, square face. Velda Mathews, aged thirty-one. All these years I had gone to groups and cultivated my inner space, hoping to find something there. Buddhism, I had tried. Psychotherapy, oh years of that. I had sat on beanbags, sobbing on strangers' shoulders and saying I loved them, but in truth it had been one big void. Then along came Kenneth and suddenly I had come alive. Ironic, wasn't it? A man who spent his time blowing people to smithereens.

I switched on the radio. It was tuned, as usual, to Radio Three, but I fiddled around until I found some news.

'*. . . a security alert in Central London . . . a soldier was shot dead in North Belfast . . .*'

I switched it off, went into the bedroom and opened the wardrobe. His clothes hung there but I couldn't touch them. I didn't want to find anything out. I went to work in a daze and served a customer with gooseberry fool instead of guacamole. Margie, who ran the café, asked if anything was the matter but I didn't tell her because once

I put it into words it would become real. Not only would I have to cope with her reaction – she adored crises – but I would have to decide what to do. Kick him out? Tell the police? Betray him, just as he had betrayed me? But maybe he had been protecting me, by his lies. You see, I didn't know how to react. My group told me how to cope with denial and rage and absence of self-worth but nobody told me how to cope with a murderer. We weren't used to that sort of thing. Parental damage was as far as we got.

He came home the next evening. He looked exhausted. We went to bed and he fell asleep, his leg a dead weight on mine. *It's dangerous, out there.* Down in the street, a police car wailed. *A man, he makes a mistake maybe once in his life and then he's caught.* Maybe he had joined when he was young and foolish, and now he could never escape. He was theirs for life, caught in a spiral of violence.

He turned over, grunting.

'If you're ever in trouble . . .' I murmured.

He sat up. 'And what trouble might that be?'

Down in the street a woman screeched with laughter. A car door slammed. I remembered my suspicions – when was it, only a week ago? Whipping a call-girl seemed such an innocent activity now. A *Carry On* film compared to this. If only I could roll back time; if only we could start again from *there*.

He went back to sleep. It was unnerving, this body next to mine. The nearest sensation was when my friend Pauline had told me she was a lesbian. The poleaxing shock . . . the slow, skin-prickling realization . . . the way I had to get to know this new Pauline all over again . . .

Suddenly I sat up. Yesterday morning, what had he been hiding from me, in the boot of his car?

I slid out of bed, wrapped myself in my kimono and crept into the hallway. I fished in his jacket pocket. How sharp and cold his keys felt, how solidly knobbly the St

25

Christopher! Actually doing something, rather than harbouring vague suspicions, is shockingly physical. I went outside. It was freezing.

I unlocked the boot and opened it. Inside, half-hidden by a blanket, was a long, bulky-looking bag. Like a bag for golf clubs, that long. Only I knew there weren't golf clubs inside.

'Can I help you?'

I swung round. A police car had drawn up beside me; I heard the crackling static of a radio.

'Just . . . forgot something in the car,' I stuttered, and slammed the boot shut.

The next morning, at seven-thirty, the phone rang. I picked it up.

'Hello?'

There was no answer, just the sound of breathing. Down the line, faintly, I heard the sound of machine-gun fire. A muffled rat-a-tat-tat. Then the receiver was replaced.

Kenneth was sitting up in bed. 'Who was that?' he asked, sharply.

'Wrong number.'

Frying his bacon, half-an-hour later, I tried to be light-hearted.

'I don't know anything about you,' I said.

'And what sort of thing might you be wanting to know, my petal?' His voice was light, too. I felt we were caught in some conspiracy together.

'Anything.' I slid the eggs onto his plate. 'I don't even know your hobbies.'

'Oh, I like to pull the wings off little girls.'

I tried to laugh. 'Well, sports then. What do you play. Tennis, golf?'

He paused. 'Golf, I enjoy. Trouble is, the people you meet.'

What did he mean – British imperialists or something? Anti-republicans? 'Do you have a club?'

'Oh no, I play with my bare hands.'

'I mean, do you belong to a club?'

He tipped the ketchup bottle; red sauce slopped onto his plate. 'The Mountview. Why, my sweetheart?'

When he had gone I looked up the Mountview Club in the Yellow Pages. It was out in Enfield. I dialled the number.

'Er, I want to leave a message for one of your members,' I said. 'A Mr Kenneth McTurk.'

There was a shuffle of paper at the other end. Somebody was obviously looking at a list. Finally the voice said: 'We have no member of that name.'

That morning explosives were found in a Ford Transit van, parked in Chancery Lane. I read about it in the *Standard*; I read the papers every day now. *Please be vigilant*, said the Head of the Anti-Terrorist Squad. *You, the public, are our eyes and ears.* There had been a spate of kidnappings in Derry, too; the latest had been a local supermarket manager and his wife. Shamefully, I didn't consider the victims in all this or the political rights and wrongs. Love makes us myopically self-absorbed. I just thought: does he really care for me, or is he using me for my flat, a place where he can lie low?

When I got home that evening he was already there; his car was parked outside in the dark street. I let myself into the flat like a thief, like somebody who didn't belong there – criminality is catching. I paused outside my bedroom door. He was talking on the phone.

'What do you mean, *now*? I can't come now!' His voice was shrill; almost unrecognizable. 'Pipe down will you! Get a hold on yourself! They'll hear what you're saying!'

I went into the kitchen and stared at the piled-up sink.

27

Ludicrously, I thought: can't even terrorists help with the washing-up? My eyes filled with tears.

'Forgive me, my lovely.'

I jumped. He was standing in the doorway. He looked terrible. His eyes were bloodshot and his tie was loose, like a drunkard's.

'I have to go out, see.'

'Why do you have to go out?' My voice rose. 'Why can't you tell me? Don't you trust me? Do you think I wouldn't understand?'

'I have no doubt whatsoever, my darling, that you wouldn't understand. Nobody in their sane mind would understand.'

He kissed me and then he left, slamming the door behind him.

I ran downstairs. His car was pulling away from the kerb, its headlight beams weeping in the rain.

At that moment I took a decision, a split-second decision; a cab was passing and I stepped into the street.

'Follow that car!' I said.

The stagey words made the whole thing unreal. I was sucked into the momentum of a thriller. I clutched my handbag to my chest, swaying as we rounded corners, jolting as we shuddered to a stop at intersections. At one point we nearly lost Kenneth, but one of his tail-lights was broken so I could spot him ahead. To calm myself I chanted 'Om, om' but it suddenly seemed silly. Had I shut the front door? Would the cats get out? Had I got enough money for the fare, wherever we were going? The driver said nothing. I watched the sturdy back of his neck; beyond it the slewing wipers and the wobbling blobs of red. They smeared, rhythmically, across the windscreen.

Half an hour passed, maybe more. Then the cab stopped. We were somewhere in the suburbs. Large, Tudor-style houses loomed up on either side. Was this IRA head-quarters? I fumbled for the fare; the driver didn't seem the slightest bit curious. Ahead of us Kenneth's car had stopped; its tail-light was extinguished. I saw him climb out, open the boot and pull out the long, heavy bag. He paused in the rain, looked up at one of the houses and walked slowly towards its front door.

I got out of the cab. The driver drove off. A woman hurried past me, her head down. I stopped her.

'Excuse me!' I hissed. 'Who lives there?'

'There?' She looked at the house. 'An estate agent.'

'Estate agent?'

'And his family.' She hurried off. I stood there, sodden.

It's odd, how one reacts in a situation like this. One can't tell beforehand, simply because it never arises. I felt disembodied, floating. Adrenalin fuelled me, like some emergency engine humming into life. I understood what was happening. He was going to kill this estate agent. Or take him hostage.

I ran towards the house. Kenneth had gone in. I rushed round the back, pushing through some wet bushes. From the ground floor came the sounds of gunfire – rat-a-tat-a-tat, machine-gun fire. I tried the kitchen door. It was open. I went in.

Upstairs I heard him shouting, and a woman's voice. 'You bastard!' she cried, over and over. 'You bastard!'

Downstairs the gunfire had stopped. I ran upstairs, two at a time. Light blazed on the landing. I heard their voices through a closed door. I flung it open.

He was standing in the bedroom with a woman. They swung round and stared at me.

'Velda!' he gasped.

'That's *her*?' said the woman. 'What's she doing here?'

My knees turned to water. I sat down, heavily, in a chair. Two boys came into the room; one of them carried a gun.

'Fergus! Dominic!' he said. 'Go back to the lounge, this minute!'

The boys looked at me, their eyes wide, and went out. Clatter-clatter went the gun against the banisters as they trailed downstairs.

The woman sat down on the bed. She was bleached blonde, and very good-looking. 'So that's her,' she said. 'She's a big girl, isn't she?'

There was a silence. Downstairs the TV came on. Kenneth, his face red, fumbled for a cheroot.

'Don't smoke that in here,' she said, 'you know I hate it.' He put the packet back in his pocket. He hung his head, like a small boy in front of a headmistress. She was looking at me with dispassionate interest. 'I didn't know anyone wore kaftans anymore.'

'Sally – '

He started to speak but she took no notice. She turned to me. 'You can have him. Do you know, Valerie or whatever it is – '

'Velda.'

' – I've actually been whistling around the house?' She flung herself back on the bed. 'Take him!' She gazed up at the chandelier. 'No more hoovering every day and keeping this huge bloody house nice, not that he'd notice, except he notices when it's not done, *and* trying to run my shop, not that I've had any support in *that* department . . .' Her voice grew dreamy. 'No more having to stop the boys fighting because it might disturb him, and clearing up their stuff but he says they should do it but if they did it it would never get done and then he'd get even more irritable, mmmm and letting them watch their ghastly videos . . .'

'I am *here*, you know,' he said.

'And he's getting so *fat*!' she said. 'It must be all those dinners he's eaten twice. First sitting chez moi and second sitting wherever you live.' She raised her head and looked at me. 'You obviously like your food too.'

'There's no need to talk to her like that!' he snapped.

She turned to him. 'I smelt a rat with that sudden interest in golf. You're such a lazy slob. Amazing I didn't guess. Tournaments in St Andrews, weekend championships God knows where. Coming back all muddy and shagged out. In a manner of speaking.' She started to laugh.

I turned to Kenneth. 'I didn't realize they were toy ones. The handcuffs.' I couldn't think of anything else to say.

'Take him!' cried Sally, tears of laughter streaming down her face. 'Take him! Make up your mind!'

A long, long moment passed. Finally I looked at Kenneth, and made up my mind.

Ta for the Memories

Edith knew nothing about pop music. For a start, she called it pop music. Apparently you were supposed to call it something else nowadays. Then there was the sight of people at pop concerts, swinging their heads round and round as if they were trying to get a crick out of their neck. Didn't they know how silly they looked? And the noise! Edith had a bicycle and a cat, both virtually silent. The only noise she made was singing in her local choir. Hayden's 'Creation' was next on the agenda.

So the name Kenny Loathsome meant nothing to her. The girls in the office moaned. 'You lucky sausage!' said Muriel in Rights. 'You'll meet him! You'll touch him! Don't wash!'

The last book Edith edited had been *Signs and Symbols in Pre-Hellenic Pottery*. That was more her thing. The publishing firm where she worked was a family business, the last of the musty old outfits in Bloomsbury. They were attempting to drag themselves into the nineties – ill-advisedly, Edith thought – by putting some glitz into their list and had signed up this Kenny Loathsome to write his autobiography.

Muriel pointed a trembling finger at her magazine. 'That's him.'

Actually, Edith did vaguely recognize him. She had videotaped a programme about Schopenhauer and got 'Top of the Pops' by mistake. With horrified fascination she had watched Kenny Loathsome snarling into a microphone – a tadpole-shaped man with disgusting hair. If *she*

35

went on TV she would wash her hair first. He was the lead singer, apparently, in a group called The Nipple Faktory. Obviously spelling wasn't one of their strong points.

'He's had sex with nine hundred women,' breathed Muriel.

'One thousand two hundred,' said Oonagh from Reception.

'Hope they kept their eyes closed,' said Edith 'and held their noses.'

So that was how she found herself flying to the Côte d'Azur, to the hideway of a famous pop star. He called it a hideaway, apparently, but you could see it for miles. It was the colour of pink blancmange and was festooned with satellite dishes. A servant-type person ushered her into Kenny Loathsome's den, a dark room lined with antique guns. He sat slumped in a leather chair watching Arsenal play Sheffield Wednesday. For half an hour this was the only information she could prise out of him. When the match was over he bellowed, either with joy or rage, and drained his tumbler of Southern Comfort. She introduced herself.

'I've come to help you write your autobiography.'

'Yeah, darling. Trouble is, I can't remember nothing.'

It was the drugs that had done it. During dinner – caviare, hamburgers and champagne – he itemized the substances he had ingested over the past twenty-five years. He said he had been a walking chemist's lab. 'Acid, speed, coke, methadone, quaaludes, diazapan.'

'My head's reeling,' she said.

'Not as much as mine was, darling.'

'What was the point of taking an upper if you were just about to take a downer?'

He said they had totally nuked his brain and the past was all a blur. The next afternoon, when he emerged blinking into the sunshine, she saw that under the hair his face was ravaged by the years of abuse. Not unattractively, actually. She had always been drawn to older men, but in the past they had been the professorial type. Back in her room she removed her glasses and put in her contact lenses.

They got down to work – well, she did. She took out her tape recorder and prodded him with questions – his childhood in Accrington, his spell as a delivery driver for a firm of wholesale butchers. 'Why are you called Loathsome?' she asked.

'Dunno.'

'Did your Mum call you that and you didn't know what it meant?'

He paused and nodded. 'Except I didn't have a Mum. It was me foster-parents.'

'Poor Kenny.' She thought of her sunlit childhood in Oxfordshire, labradors and sisters and Marmite sandwiches. No wonder he didn't want to remember.

He sat there, his face furrowed with concentration. 'Think!' she ordered. 'Martial said "To be able to enjoy one's past life is to live twice." '

'Martial? What team does he play for?'

'You must remember something. What sort of delivery van did you drive?' she asked. 'Who were your friends at school?'

He spoke stumblingly. After her second glass of Rémy Martin she said recklessly: 'If you can't remember, make it up!' She was an *editor*. What was happening to her?

He kept depraved, nocturnal hours, getting up at noon and staying up till late. At three in the morning, yawning, she switched off the tape recorder. 'Could you ever sing at all? Did you have any talent whatsoever?'

He shook his head.

'Funny, isn't it,' she said. 'You can't sing and you're a millionaire. I've got a beautiful voice and I'm broke.'

He laughed his gravelly laugh, choking in his cigarette smoke. 'And who's the happiest little camper?'

A week went by and he didn't make a pass at her. What was wrong? She put up her hair but he didn't seem to notice; her eyes stung from her blithering contact lenses. She wasn't sure she wanted him to try but her pride was at stake. What was she going to tell them back in the office? He seemed to live in a state of amiable, alcoholic stupefaction. Whilst she transcribed her tapes he watched satellite game shows or spent hours on the phone to his business manager. He was suing his band for some recording deal (note that she now said 'band' not group). He tussled with faxes about alimony suits and palimony suits. All the worry had given him a peptic ulcer. No, nothing happened. The most exciting event in her bedroom was when she dropped a contact lens and, blindly searching for it, knocked against the panic button and summoned a vanload of *gendarmes* from Nice.

The only things he really loved were his vintage cars. He took her into his triple garage where they slumbered under dustsheets. 'Feel that bodywork!' he said, stroking the sleek flank of an Alvis or something. 'She's, like, responsive, know what I mean? She don't want nothing from me – like, me house in Berkshire and half me assets. That's why I love her, see?' He sighed. 'Dynamite when she's warmed up. 'Cept I've lost me driving licence.'

'You could always get a bike,' said Edith briskly. She was beginning to suspect that his legendary conquests were as much a fabrication as the past they had been cobbling together in the gloom of his den.

In two weeks they were finished. As she waited for her taxi he ruffled her hair. 'Take care, darling,' he said. 'See you around.' Around where? Nowhere *she* went.

She arrived back in London looking radiant. That fortnight had changed her in a way nobody could guess. At

the rehearsal that night her voice soared. Next day she
met a breathless reception in the office.

'Your tan! You look great without your glasses! Go on,
tell us. What happened? Did you . . .?'

Edith smiled mysteriously. She dumped her transcripts
on her desk. She looked at the heap of paper. She had
given him a past; she had created it for him. He was
grateful to her and in a curious way she was grateful to
him. So why couldn't he create a past for her? For didn't
Alexander Smith say 'A man's real possession is his
memory. In nothing else is he rich, in nothing else is he
poor.' (*Dreamthorpe* 1863)

'Oh, it was extraordinary all right.' She sipped her Nescafé, gazing at the pairs of round eyes. She was Sheheraz-
ade, she was all-powerful. 'He was even better than all
the stories.'

'How? What did he do? Did he, you know . . .?'

She nodded, she sipped, she took her time. 'We stayed
up all night. We didn't get up till lunchtime.'

'What did he do?'

'He stroked my flanks, his eyes full of desire. He murmured "How responsive you are . . . when you're warmed
up, you're dynamite!" '

They sighed, like a breeze through pine trees.

'We went up to my room. Our lovemaking was so
intense that we rolled off the bed and I hit his panic
button . . . half the Nice *gendarmerie* arrived . . . As George
Dennison Prentice said – '

'Who?'

'In his *Prenticiana*: "Memory is not so brilliant as hope,
but it is more beautiful, and a thousand times as true." '

She wasn't sure about this, but they didn't seem to
notice.

Soon after that the firm was bought by a multi-national
media conglomerate which owned six satellite TV stations

and Edith was made redundant. Her tan had long since faded. She went to work for a professor of Middle English who was writing a book called *Courtly Love: Legend and Myth*. Which had she created – legend or myth? Did she actually know, or care? She only knew she was grateful to Kenny Loathsome and he would never know why. For he had made her happy with her two rooms in Peckham High Street, and besides, it was simpler to be loved by her cat.

The next September his book was published. She heard he was doing a signing in Harrods so she went there and queued. It was all women, nudging and giggling. When she finally got to his table he didn't recognize her. She knew he wouldn't. His head was bent down as he wrote, laboriously. She noticed, for the first time, that he was thinning on top.

'What shall I write, love?' he asked, without looking up.

She smiled, and pointed to the empty page. 'Just write "Ta for the memories." '

Stopping at the Lights

I saw Scottie today. I was stopped at some traffic lights and I saw his little face, quite clearly. When he grinned, that's when I knew. But there were cars behind me, honking.

I've still got the bit of paper from his Dad. It's somewhere, I know it is. Tonight I'm going to have a really good look. Wigan, I think he's gone. I'm meeting this bloke tonight, 7 p.m. outside Garfunkel's. He's from Computer Dateline, so I bet I'll be home early. I'll look then.

Off and on all day I've been thinking about him. Scottie, I mean. He was such a gorgeous kid. Ginger hair, freckly nose. Racing around going vroom-vroom. He arrived with his mum four years ago and they moved into Trailer Four. They didn't have a car; they must have walked from the bus stop with their suitcases, the wind blowing off the fens like knives. His mum, Janine, was very young but she always wore high heels. Mottled, bare legs, but always a pair of slingbacks. Ankle-chain, too. Looking at her face, you wouldn't think she was a goer. Mousy little thing, undernourished. It was like all the vibrancy had drained into her footwear. And into her son; he was bouncing with life.

I never knew where they came from, but that wasn't so unusual in those days. My husband, Jim, asked no questions. He didn't ask *me* many questions, either. To tell the truth, he didn't talk much at all, except to his budgies. He bred pieds and opalines; he played them Radio One.

43

He stood in their aviary for hours, squirting his champion hens with plume spray.

Graceland, that's what our place was called. After The King, of course. It was a little bungalow outside Spalding. There were ploughed fields either side, as far as you could see. It was dead flat. The road outside ran straight as a ruler. We had half an acre out the back, conifers fencing it in, and it was there that the trailers were parked. Seven of them. At night you could see the seven blue glows from their TVs. Sometimes, when I was feeling fidgety, I'd walk around at night; I could follow the story in *Miami Vice*, the actors mouthing at me.

I could hear the sneezes, too; the walls were that thin. And the rows, of course. There were always people coming and going, cars starting up in the middle of the night. That's why Jim insisted on rent in advance, and deposits on the calor gas cylinders. Our tenants told me such stories about their lives and I always believed them. Mr Pilcher, who said he was just stopping for a week or so while a loan came through from the Chase Manhattan Bank. Mr Carling, who said the girl he was living with was his wife, though I heard her, quite clearly once, call him 'Dad'. The bloke who said he was a Yemeni prince before they took him back to the hospital. Sometimes the police arrived, Sheba barking, blue lights flashing around our lounge. When Mr Mason did a flit, for instance. He told me he owned a copper mine in the Cameroons but when they opened up his trailer it was full of these videos. I nicked one; I thought it might re-activate our sex life, but I just got the giggles and Jim was shocked. He was much older than me, you see; he liked to believe I was innocent. He wouldn't listen to those stories of Elvis getting bloated either. Who was I, to tell him the truth? I was in a real mess when he took me in, he was ever so good to me. I loved Jim, I really did, though I did behave badly on occasions. But he always took me back, no questions asked. He didn't want to hear.

Janine was running away from something, I could tell, because she never got any letters. Nobody knew she was there. But then nobody knew that most of our tenants were there. It was as if we didn't exist.

'Know what we are?' I said to Jim one night. 'Lincolnshire's answer to the Bermuda Triangle. We're the place people disappear to.'

We were playing Travel Scrabble; he was trying to enlarge his vocabulary. 'FYRED', he put down, smoke wreathing up between his fingers. He had been a heavy smoker since he was fourteen, and ran away to join the Wall of Death.

'It's not Y,' I chortled, 'it's I.'

'I know it's you,' he said, stroking my cheek with his nicotine-stained finger. 'Every morning, I can't believe my luck.'

After that, I hadn't the heart to correct him.

Janine was a hopeless mother. At that period there happened to be no other kids around; Scottie was bored, but I never saw her playing with him. She sat on the steps of her trailer, painting her toenails and reading the fiction pull-outs in women's magazines. Sometimes she tottered up the road in her high heels and stopped at the phone box. Once she dyed a whole load of clothes mulberry and hung them up to dry; they flapped in the wind like whale skins. She hadn't a clue about cooking; then neither had I. Sometimes, suddenly, she decided to make something impossible like angel cakes. 'Can I borrow a recipe book?' she'd say, but I only had the manual that came with my microwave. Domesticity wasn't our *forte*. But surely, I thought, if *I* had a kid I'd be better at it?

Scottie liked wandering into our bungalow. He liked tapping on the aquarium and making the guppies jump. He liked inspecting Jim's trophies from the Cage Bird

Society. He liked sitting on my knee, pulling bits of fluff out of my sweater and telling me stories. 'My Dad's an airline pilot,' he said one day. The next time his Dad would be a champion boxer. I'd be lying under my sun lamp and there he would be, staring at me with that clear, frank look kids have.

'Why're you doing that?' he said.

'Got to be ready for when the limo arrives,' I said, my eyes closed behind my goggles. 'It's a stretch, see. Cocktail cabinet and all. Got to be ready for Tom Cruise.'

One day he came in when Jim had got dressed up in his Elvis gear. It was the white satin outfit – slashed shirt, rhinestones, the works. Jim was going to the Elvis Convention in Coventry. I was embarrassed – I was always embarrassed when Jim looked like that – but Scottie didn't mind. Besides, he was togged up too, in his cowboy suit. I looked at them in their fancy dress: the six-year-old Lone Ranger and the fifty-year-old Elvis with his wizened, gypsy face and bowed legs.

'My Dad's a famous pop singer,' said Scottie.

'Is he now?' asked Jim, inspecting himself in the mirror. He combed back his hair to cover his bald patch.

'He's so famous I'm not allowed to say his name,' said Scottie. 'My Dad's got a Gold Disc.'

'Know how many he's got?' Jim pointed to the Elvis medallion on the wall. 'Fifty-one. The most awards to an individual in history. Fifty-one Gold Discs.'

I laughed. 'Know what Jim's got? A slipped disc.'

They both swung round and stared at me. I blushed. I hadn't meant to say that; it had just popped out. Jim turned away. He knelt down and adjusted Scottie's bootlace tie.

I tried to make it better. 'He got it on the Wall of Death,' I said. 'Riding the motorbikes. You know he worked on it? He was the champion for years. They went all over – Strathclyde, Farnham. Till he did his back in.'

Neither of them replied. Jim was kneeling beside Scottie,

re-buckling his holster belt. 'Wrong way round, mate,' he said.

Eight months passed. Scottie didn't go to school. Sooner or later, I thought, somebody in authority was going to catch up with him and his mother. She looked restless, laying out Tarot cards on her steps and then suddenly sweeping them all into a pile. Sometimes she tottered up the road and just stood there at the bus stop, looking at the timetable. I dreaded Scottie going. I loved having him around, even though he got up to all sorts of mischief. One day I caught him opening the aviary door. Luckily the budgies just sat there on their perches, the dozy buggers. They were that dim. God knows what Jim used to find to say to them.

At our place, see, people came and went; they never stayed for long. Eight months was about the limit, for us. I remember one evening, when I was waiting for my highlights to take – I was wearing one of those hedgehog caps – I remember saying to Jim: 'It's like, this place, we're like traffic lights. People just stop here for a while, you never know where they've been or where they're going. The lights turn green and whoosh! They fuck off.'

I think he replied but I couldn't hear, the rubber cap was over my ears, but it was true. We were just a stopping place at some dodgy moment in people's lives, people who were trying to make it to London one day, when their luck changed. Or maybe they were escaping from London, from something in their past, and they fetched up with us. I had a friend in London, Mandie; she and I had this dream of setting up our own little hairdressing business one day.

People came and went, and there Jim and I were, grounded on East Fen Road with our broken cars. Jim had these cars out in the front yard, you see – Cadillacs and things, Pontiacs, American cars, the sort you saw in films

47

with Sandra Dee in them, and despite his arthritis he spent all day underneath them, tinkering with their innards, while his beloved Country and Western songs played on his portable cassette recorder.

Scottie liked to sit in the cars too. He would sit there for hours, waggling the steering wheel and making humming noises through his lips. He was in a world of his own, he was going anywhere in the world. When he climbed out he wiped his hands on his jeans, like Jim wiped his hands on his overalls when they were greasy; his face had that set, important look blokes have when it's a job well done, that nobody else would understand.

In July there was a heatwave. Janine grew jittery, like a horse smelling a thunderstorm. I woke up one night and saw her standing in the dark, ghostly in her white nightie against the solid black of the cypress trees. The moon shone on her upturned face.

The next morning it was very hot. There was a tap on my back door and there she stood, thin and pale in her halter-neck top. She never got tanned, even in that heat, and even though I had offered her unlimited sessions under my lamp. Her face was tight; just for a moment I thought that something terrible had happened.

She said: 'It's Scottie's birthday today and he's set his little heart on meringues.'

'Why didn't you tell me? I want to get him a present!'

'Is Jim going into Spalding? He could give me a lift and I'll buy some.'

But Jim had removed the carburettor from the Capri, our only roadworthy car; bits of dismembered metal lay all over the yard. We were marooned.

So we decided to have a go at cooking the meringues ourselves. I phoned up my friend Gloria, who was trained in catering, she did the lunches at the King's Head, and she told me the recipe. Egg whites, icing sugar, easy-peasy but keep the oven really low, Mark One.

Easy-peasy it wasn't. Janine had run out of calor gas, see, so we whisked up the egg whites and put them on a baking tray in my own oven. Just then we heard a bellow from Trailer One. Mr Parker's TV had gone dead. He used to sit in there all day watching TV, and it was in the middle of Gloria Hunniford when the electricity went off. We were always having power cuts.

Nobody else was home that day except Mr Parker. We couldn't use his calor gas cooker. I'd only been in his trailer the once and, to put it mildly, hygienic wasn't the first word that sprang to mind. Besides, he was always trying to lift my skirt with his walking stick.

So know what I did? I put the tray of meringues into the Ford Capri. It was at least 120 degrees in there. I put the baking tray on the back seat and closed the door. 'Aren't I a genius?' I said, polishing an imaginary lapel. 'I'm wasted here.'

We suddenly got the giggles. Even Jim joined in.

'One oven, fully MOT'd,' I said.

'It's Meals on Wheels,' said Jim.

'Change into fourth,' said Janine 'to brown it nicely on top.'

Jim was chuckling so much that he started one of his coughing fits. Scottie jumped up and down. Sheba's chain rattled as she ran this way and that, suddenly sitting down and thumping her tail.

While the meringues were cooking in the car I went indoors, to find Scottie a present. I went into the bedroom. All my soft toys were there, heaped up on the bed – teddies, rabbits, the giraffe from my twenty-first. I liked to cuddle them at night. I picked up Blinge, my koala bear, and paused. It was as if I was seeing them for the first time. They made me feel awkward, as if I was intruding on myself. They were too babyish for Scottie.

Just then Jim came in. He had recovered from his coughing fit and he was mopping his forehead. He opened the wardrobe and looked in. He always took his time. Then he took out his cowboy hat.

It was still wrapped in plastic. You should have seen it: palest tan, with a woven suede band around the brim. The genuine article. He had bought it at a country and western event in Huddersfield and it had cost a fortune.

'Oh Jim,' I breathed.

'Got any wrapping paper?' he asked.

We had a wonderful party, the four of us. Looking back, maybe we all felt that something was about to happen. At the time I just thought it was the rush you get with a birthday, the jolt it gives you. The fridge had rumbled back to life and we drank cans of Budweiser and a bottle of German wine. Janine and Jim, who had hardly spoken all those months, even danced together to Tammy Wynette, crooning the soppy lyrics. Jim was supposed to be off the booze, but to tell the truth it improved him. Janine's sallow face was flushed. I danced with Scottie, the cowboy hat slipping over his nose. In the middle we suddenly remembered our meringues. We rushed out and opened the back door of the Capri. They hadn't cooked; they had just sort of subsided. It didn't matter. We gave them to Sheba, our canine dustbin.

When the sun went down we sat on the back porch. Janine put her arm around her son and squeezed him. She wasn't usually demonstrative.

'You're a big boy now,' she said, 'you're the man of the family.'

'He's not big,' I said. 'He's only a kid.'

She squeezed him tighter. 'You'll look after me. You'll see it's all OK.'

'At seven?' I asked. 'Give him a chance!'

There was a silence. From the trailers came the murmur of TVs, the rising laughter of a canned audience. Beyond the bungalow, we heard cars whizzing past on the road. Where were they going?

Jim spoke. He said: 'I wish to God I'd had a son.'

That was the first and last time he ever spoke of it.

The next morning I was standing in the kitchen, looking at the bowl of egg yolks. Six egg yolks; what was I supposed to do with them? I was standing there when the phone rang.

A woman's voice asked: 'Is there a J. Maddox at that address please?'

'Nobody of that name,' I replied. It was so hot that the receiver stuck to my hand.

'Are you sure about that? Janine Maddox?'

I paused. Janine's surname was Smith. That's what she had told us, anyway. We got a lot of Smiths.

Something in the woman's voice made me wary. 'Sorry,' I said, 'nobody of that name here.'

A fly buzzed against the window pane. Outside, in the yard, Scottie was sitting in the Chevrolet. It was his favourite. I could just see the top of his head, at the wheel. Jim had managed to get the electrics working and Scottie was trying out the indicators. First the left one winked: that way it was London. Then the right one: that meant somewhere else, somewhere beyond my calculations. Somewhere only Scottie knew.

I suddenly felt sad. I went out the back. Janine had washed her hair. She sat on the steps of her trailer, her hair wrapped in a towelling turban, smoking. For once there was no sign of a magazine. I realized for the first time that she was ever so young – twenty-two, maybe. Twenty-three. Younger than me. I realized that I hardly knew anything about her.

51

'Someone just phoned,' I said, 'asking about you.'

Her head jerked up. 'Who was it?'

'A woman,' I replied. 'It's all right. I said I didn't know you.'

She looked down at her feet. They were bare today, but her scuffed white slingbacks were lying on the grass nearby. When her toes were squashed into them, Scottie said they looked like little maggots.

She blew out smoke, shrugging her bony shoulders. 'Thanks,' she said.

There was a thunderstorm that night. I lay next to Jim, listening to his wheezing breaths. His lungs creaked like a door, opening and closing. My koala, Blinge, was pressed between us; my giraffe, Estelle, lay on the other side. She took up as much room as another person. I could feel her plush hoof resting against my thigh.

Outside, the sky rumbled. It sounded like furniture being shifted. It sounded like bulky objects being dragged across tarmac. I lay there drowsily. I've always loved thunderstorms; when I was little I used to crawl into bed with my mum and smell her warm body smells.

Maybe, in fact, that noise *was* something being moved. At our place, things were often shifted at night. The thunder cracked. I touched Blinge's leather nose. 'It's all right,' I whispered, 'it's nothing.' I ran my finger over his glass eye; there was only one left. 'I'm here.'

Jim stirred in his sleep. He wheezed, and then there was a silence. It went on for an alarmingly long time. I held my breath, willing the noises to start again.

Finally they did; the creaking wheezes. I wrapped my arm around his gaunt chest. He muttered something in his sleep; I couldn't catch the words. Then he said, quite distinctly: 'You've got your life waiting.'

The next morning Janine and Scottie had gone. Cleared

out. Their trailer was empty. We never knew who had come to collect them, moving their belongings in the night, or where they had gone. All that remained were small mementoes of Scottie: his sweet wrappers, swept into a corner of the trailer – Janine was surprisingly tidy, she wasn't like me in that respect. A criss-cross of knife marks in the trunk of one of the cypress trees, as if he were going to start a game of noughts and crosses, and hadn't found anybody to play them with.

Not long after that, a few months in fact, they demolished our place to build an out-of-town shopping mall. A socking great thing, with an atrium – they're all the rage. It was called the Rushy Dyke Shopping Experience. Rushy Dyke made me giggle; it sounded like a lesbian in a hurry. Despite my sojourn in the fens I hardly knew that dyke meant ditch. To tell the truth, I'd hardly stepped a hundred yards up the road. If you had seen our locality you would understand. No point walking somewhere when you can see exactly where you're going, is there?

Our property, where we lived, that's where the access road is now. They've put up traffic lights, too, it's that congested. So I was proved right. Graceland, and its accompanying trailer park, was just a brief stopping place for all concerned.

I got a job at the Rushy Dyke Shopping Experience. Jim was in hospital by then, and I visited him in the evenings, en route to my flat above one of Spalding's hot spots, Paradise Video Rentals. Sitting beside my storage heater I grieved for my husband, whilst the local ravers visited the premises below, hiring videos with Bruce Willis in them. The manager, Keith, watched the latest releases all evening, gunfire erupting through my carpet. It was as if Scottie was downstairs, shooting everything in sight. Then the shop went quiet, and I was alone. I thought of Jim, wheezing beside me in the night. I thought of him more than he ever believed.

I'll tell you about my job. I stood under the atrium bit, glass arches above me as high as a cathedral. One side of me there was a Next; the other side there was a Body Shop. It was nice and warm, that was something. Canned music played, to put people into the mood. It never rained there, and the wind never blew like knives. They had invented new street names and put up the signs: Tulip Walk, Daffodil Way. That was because Spalding is famous for bulbs.

I had to wear: Item One – a mob cap. Item Two – a gingham apron. The first day I felt a right prat. I stood at a farm cart in the middle of the mall, selling Old Ma Hodge's Butterscotch Bonbons. They were packaged in little cardboard cottages, with flowers printed on them. Actually the bonbons were made in a factory in Walsall but who was I to tell? Maureen, who became my friend, she stood at an adjacent cart selling Country Fayre Pot Pourris. Know them? Those things full of dead petals nobody knows what to do with. Both enterprises were leased on a franchise basis to a man we never saw, called Mr Ranesh.

I only worked there for a year, while Jim was holding on for longer than anyone had expected. He had always been stubborn. Now he couldn't speak so well, he suddenly seemed to have a lot to say. On my visits he told me more than I had heard in five years of marriage to him. It was mostly about his early days in children's homes. He spoke in a rush, kneading my fingers.

At work I re-arranged my wares, stacking up my toffee cottages and signalling by semaphore to Maureen, who was going through a divorce. She crouched behind her cart reading a book called *Life Changes – a User's Guide*. She said we were in the same boat, but I didn't agree.

*

I never knew what the weather was like outside, so I can't recall what season it was when the man came in. He wore a two-tone turquoise anorak, so maybe it was winter. He looked lost; he didn't look as if he had come in to do any shopping. We didn't get many single blokes there, except at Discount Digital Tectonics; most blokes were simply being towed along by their wife and kids.

I saw him approaching Maureen, at the next cart. She flirted with him and flashed me a glance. A man! He spoke to her for a moment, then she pointed to me. He came over.

'Douglas McLaughlan,' he said, extending his hand. He was a beefy bloke, not unattractive. Ginger hair and twinkly eyes. Sort of jaunty. Despite the name, he had a London accent. 'The charming young lady over there thought you might be able to help me.' He cleared his throat. 'I believe you have connections with a caravan park hereabouts.'

'Me and my husband ran it,' I said. 'It was right here, where you're standing. But they knocked it down to build this.'

He paused, taking this in. 'Ah,' he said. He offered me a small cigar. A woman passed, pushing a pair of twins in a double buggy. A group of schoolgirls came out of the Body Shop, linking arms. 'I'm looking for a young lady called Janine,' he said. Then he added casually: 'And her little lad.'

It was then that I realized. I looked at him, recognizing the likeness. The ginger hair, of course. He had Scottie's freckles, too, and his jutting lower lip. Scottie's lip had that determined look when he was concentrating on his driving.

'I'm sorry,' I said, 'I haven't a clue where they've gone.'

He smoked in silence for a moment.

'I'm sorry,' I said again. I felt awkward, and re-arranged the cottages.

'Had to do a bit of travelling,' he said, 'what with one

thing and another. Thought I'd found them this time. Thought I'd hit the jackpot.'

I looked up. 'He was a gorgeous kid.'

'He was?'

I nodded. The man took out a piece of paper and wrote something down. 'If you hear anything . . .' He said something about going to Wigan. Then he handed the paper to me. 'Funny old business, isn't it.'

We stood there for a moment. Then he pointed, with his thumb, at the little cardboard cottages. Sometimes, when I was bored, I arranged them into streets like a real village. He pointed at the display trays featuring the smiling face of Old Ma Hodge in her broderie anglaise bonnet.

'Don't believe a word of it myself,' he said. 'Do you?'

I drive a Sunbeam Alpine now; it's a collector's item. First thing I did, when I came to London, was learn to drive. I whizz all over London, fixing people's hair in their own homes. I started on my friend Mandie's hair, and some of the blokes at the club where she works, and the word got round. I'm quite good, you see. I tell my new clients that I trained at Michaeljohn's and I believe it myself now. Jim believed he worked on the Wall of Death even though he only drove the equipment lorry. His real name was Arnold, in fact, but he re-christened himself after Jim Reeves, another of his heroes. I only learnt this near the end. With all the harm in the world, what's the harm in that? Scottie never knew his father; he can believe anything.

I was thinking this today, because I saw him. I told you, didn't I? I saw Scottie when I was sitting at the lights.

It was at a junction leading into the Euston Road. These two boys were there, teenagers really, washing windscreens. They started on mine before I could stop them. There was a lot of splashing and lather. I think they liked the car; you don't see many Sunbeams around nowadays.

Anyway I sat there, flustered, rooting around for a 50p piece.

They did it really thoroughly, there was foam all over the place. Then suddenly, as the lights changed, the windscreen was wiped clear and I saw his face. He was wearing a denim jacket and a red t-shirt; there were pimples on his chin, as well as freckles. I only realized who he was after I had wound down the window and passed him the coin. 'Cheers,' he said. His piping voice had broken.

The cars behind me were blaring their horns. I had to move on. I was helpless in the three lanes of traffic, like a stick in a rushing current, there was a socking great lorry thundering behind me.

It took me a while to get back to where I'd begun. It was the same place, I know it was – big office block one side, church the other, covered with plastic sheets and scaffolding. It was the same place, all right. But the boys had gone.

Not a trace. They must have picked up their bucket and gone. There was nothing left except some damp patches on the tarmac.

Gentlemen always sleep on the damp patch. I suddenly thought of Jim, and how he winced when I said something crude like that. I thought of how he had been a gentleman all his life, with nobody to tell him how.

The lights changed to green. I thought of how he never blamed me for the one thing I couldn't give him. Then the chorus of horns started up behind me, and I had to move on.

How I Learnt to be a Real Countrywoman

We were sitting in the kitchen, opening Christmas cards. There was one from Sheila and Paul, whoever they were, and one from our bank manager, and one from my Aunt Aurora which had been recycled from the year before. The last one was a brown envelope. Edwin opened it.

'My God!' he said. 'These bureaucrats have a charming sense of timing.' He tugged at his beard – a newly-acquired mannerism. Since we had moved to the country he had grown a beard; it made him look like Thomas Carlyle. I hadn't told him this because he would think I was making some sort of point.

The letter was from our local council, and it said they were going to build a ring road right through our local wood.

Now Beckham Wood wasn't up to much, but it was all we had. It was more a copse, really, across the field from our cottage. Like everything in the country it was surrounded by barbed wire, but I could worm my way through with the children, and amid acres of ploughed fields it was at least somewhere to go, and from which we could then proceed home again. Such places are necessary with small children (eight, six and three).

It was mostly brambles, and trees I couldn't name because I had always lived in London. There was a small, black pond; it smelt like damp laundry one has forgotten about in the back of a cupboard. Not a lot grew in the wood, except Diet Pepsi cans and objects which my children thought were balloons until I distracted their attention. But I loved it, and now I knew it was condemned I appreciated its tangled rustlings, just as one listens most intently to a person who is going to die.

'A two-lane dual carriageway!' said Edwin. 'Right past our front door. Thundering pantechnicons!' This exploded from him like an oath. It *was* an oath. He went off to work, and every time the kids broke something that morning, which was frequently, we cried 'Thundering pantechnicons!' But that wasn't going to keep them away.

We live in a pretty, but not pretty enough to be protected, part of Somerset. People were going to campaign against this ring road, but the only alternative was through our MP's daughter's riding school, so there wasn't much hope.

That afternoon I drove off to look for holly. When you live in the country you spend your whole life in the car. In London, of course, you simply buy holly at your local shops, which is much better for the environment. I spent two hours burning up valuable fossil fuels, the children squabbling over their crisps in the back seat, and returned with only six sprigs, most of whose berries had fallen off by the time we had hung them up.

This was our first Christmas in the country, the first of our new pure life, and I was trying to work up a festive spirit unaided by the crass high-street commercialism that Edwin was so relieved to escape. Me too, of course.

Have you noticed how dark it gets, and how soon, in the country? When I returned home our wood was simply a denser clot against the sodium glow of our local town, the one whose traffic congestion was going to be eased at our expense. This time next Christmas, I thought, the thundering pantechnicons will be rattling our window panes and filling our rooms with lead pollution. It will be just like Camden Town all over again, but without the conversation.

That was what I missed, you see. Edwin didn't because he has inner resources. He's the only person I have ever met who has actually read *The Faerie Queene*. He has a spare, linear mind and fine features; nobody would ever, ever think of calling him Ed. When we lived in London, in Camden Town, he taught graphics. But then his art school was dissolved into another one and he lost his job. The government was brutish and philistine and London was full of fumes, so he said we should move to the country and I followed in the hot slipstream of his despair.

'Look at the roses growing in our children's cheeks!' he cried out, startling me, soon after we moved.

It was all right for him. He had people to talk to. He became a carpenter – sorry, Master Joiner – and he worked with two men, all of them bearded. The other two were called Piers and Marcus; they were that up-market. They toiled in a barn, looking like an illustration in my old *Golden Book of Bible Stories*, while Fats Waller played on their cassette recorder. They made very expensive and uncomfortable wooden furniture. Thank goodness we couldn't afford it. It was Shaker-style, like the furniture in *Witness*, which I had already rented three times from our visiting video van because all his other films were Kung Fu. The van came on Wednesdays and its driver, an ex-pig-farmer with a withered arm, was sometimes the only adult I spoke to all day, unless someone came to buy our eggs, which was hardly ever.

I talked to the hens, of course, and to the children. I had also become a secret addict of *Neighbours*, which ended just before Edwin arrived home each day, though he probably heard its soppy theme tune as he took off his bicycle clips. I never dreamed I would work out who all the characters were, they all looked the same, pan-sticked under the arc lights with their streaky perms, but to my shame I did, and worse, I minded. I even hummed its tune when I was standing at the sink, digging all the slugs out of our organic vegetables.

Perhaps, I thought, if I joined the anti-road campaign I

could meet intelligent men like Jonathon Porritt. Perhaps they didn't all live in NW1. Most of them seemed to; that was the trouble. I missed Camden Town, where everyone worked in the media. At the children's primary school, where they had cutbacks, parents donated scrap paper and they were always things like shooting scripts for *The South Bank Show*. I used to read them, on the other side of the children's drawings, so I could startle Edwin when we were watching TV and I knew what Leonard Bernstein was going to say. Then there was the time when I could tell him who did the murder in a Ruth Rendell book, because I had found the last page in our local photocopier. Edwin thought all this was febrile, but Edwin had inner resources. I only had the children. You can't have both.

And then, on Boxing Day, I had a brainwave.

It was freezing outside and the cat had had an accident in front of the Aga. Well, not an accident; she just hadn't bothered to go outside. Edwin was clearing it up with some newspaper when he stopped, and read a corner.

'Listen to this,' he said. 'Leicester County Council is spending £19,000 on four underpasses, specially constructed for wildlife.'

At the time I wasn't listening. I was throwing old roast potatoes into the hen bucket and working out how long it had been since Edwin and I had made love.

'It's to save a colony of Great Crested Newts,' he said.

We hadn't even on Christmas night, after some wonderful oak-aged Australian Cabernet Sauvignon. The last time had been Thursday week, when we had been agreeing how awful his mother was. This always drew us close. For such a pure-minded man he could get quite bitchy, when we talked about her, and this invigorated us. We had one or two such mild but reliable aphrodisiacs. Usually, however, our feet were too cold, or one of the children suddenly woke up or we had just been reading something depressing about the hole in the ozone layer.

Then I thought about the campaign, and as he started washing the floor I caught up with what he had said about the newts.

It was such a simple idea, so breathtakingly simple that my legs felt boneless and I had to sit down.

I didn't know much about natural history when all this happened, last Christmas. I was brought up in Kensington and spent my childhood with my nose pressed against shop windows, first toys then bikes then clothes. Unlike Edwin, I have always been an enthusiastic member of the consumer society. If a bird was brown and boring I presumed it was a sparrow. Frogs were simply pear-shaped diagrams of reproductive organs which we sniggered over in biology lessons.

Then Edwin and I married and we went to live in Camden Town. Its streets were bedimmed with sulphuric emissions and we could only recognize the changing seasons by the daffodil frieze at Sketchleys (spring) and the Back-to-Skool promotion at Rymans (autumn). In our local park litter lay like fallen blossoms all year round. Edwin, waking up to a dawn chorus of activated car alarms, hungered for honest country toil and started buying books, published by Faber and illustrated by woodcuts, which told him how to clamp his beetroots and flay his ox.

A romantic puritan, he bemoaned the greed of our decade, saying that even intellectuals seemed to talk about house prices nowadays. He said London was so materialistic, so cut off from Real Values. We lived in a flat, and my contact with nature was to grow basil, the seventies herb, and coriander, the eighties one, on our balcony, digging them with a dining fork. I bought them at Clifton Nurseries, London's most metropolitan garden centre, where I liked spotting TV personalities pushing Burnham Woods of designer foliage in their trolleys to the checkout.

So I came to the country green, as it were. And after a

year of organic gardening all I had learnt was how to drive into Taunton, buy most of the stuff at Marks and Spencers and then pretend it was ours. It's so tiring, being organic. Being married, for that matter.

The day after Boxing Day I walked across to the wood, alone. It was a still, grey morning and without its foliage the place looked thin and vulnerable; I could see right through it. Within its brambles was now revealed the archaeological remains of countless trysts, date-expired litter from expired dates. But now I knew what I was doing I felt possessive. We didn't own the wood, of course – it belonged to our local farmer, Mr Hogben, and he wanted the ring road because it meant he could retire to Portugal.

I took out my rubbish bags and set to work. It's amazing how much you can do when you don't have three children with you. In an hour I had tut-tutted my way through the place, filled four black bags, and scratched my hands.

That evening I didn't watch TV. I looked through Edwin's library instead. He was outside, in the old privy, running off campaign leaflets on his printing press. Nursing my burning hands I leafed through his *Complete British Wild Flowers*. I had no idea there were so many plants, and with such names – Sneezewort and Dodder, Purging Buckthorn and Bitter Fleabane, Maids Bonnets and Biting Stonecrop (or Welcome-Home-Husband-Though-Never-So-Drunk). Poetic and unfamiliar, they danced in my head as I gazed at the eternally-blooming watercolours. The book divided them into habitats, which helped. I took note of the 'Woodlands' section, writing down the names of the most endangered species. I hadn't learnt so much since school.

When Edwin returned he was suprised I was missing *Minder*. So was I.

'I want to learn more about the countryside,' I said.

He was terribly pleased. We started talking about his

youth in Dorset, where his father was a vicar and he a pale, only child. He told me how he had wandered around with a stick, poking holes in cowpats.

'I became an expert on spotting those in perfect condition. Crusty on top, but still soft inside. A pitiful little skill, but something, I suppose . . .' He paused. 'Other people remember their childhoods as always being sunny. All I can remember is the rain. Sitting for hours at the window, looking at it sliding down the pane.' He looked at me. 'I wish you'd been there, I wish I knew you then.'

'Do you?'

'You'd have thought of lots of things to do.'

I was moved by this; it was the first time he had admitted to being bored. Unhappy maybe, but never bored. People like *me* were bored by the countryside. We talked about the treacherous nature of expectations. We talked about the years before graphics department politics, and children, and trying to find people rich enough to buy his tables.

'I wanted to be Edward Lear,' he said. 'I wanted to explore the world and find everything curious.'

'Not just cow-pats,' I said. 'But wasn't he lonely?'

He nodded. 'But what an artist.' He paused, tugging his beard. 'Everybody has a time when they should have lived.'

'When's yours?'

'1890.'

'Think about how much it would have hurt at the dentist's.'

He laughed. 'When's yours?'

'Now.'

That night, despite our icy feet, we made love – the first time since that Thursday. He even licked my ears, something I had forgotten I adored. He used to do it quite a lot, in London.

Afterwards he said: 'I've been worried about you,

Ruthie. Have I been dominating? Selfish? Bringing you down here?'

I shook my head. 'I'm liking it better now.'

Mabel Cudlipp had newts. She was a fellow mother. I had seen her at the school gates for a year now but we had never really talked. To tell the truth, I thought the mothers here looked boring compared with the London ones, who arrived at school breathing chardonnay fumes from Groucho lunches. But when the spring term began I started chatting, and it turned out Mabel Cudlipp had some in her pond.

'Great Crested Newts,' she said. 'They're very rare. In fact, they've been protected since 1981.'

'You couldn't possibly spare one or two?'

She nodded. 'They're hibernating now, but we can look when it gets warmer.'

So then she introduced herself, and she even brought her daughter back for tea.

You might wonder why I didn't tell Edwin. The trouble was: his honesty. Once, he found a £5 note in Oxford Circus and took it to the police. They were as taken aback as I was. Nobody claimed it, of course, because nobody thought anyone could be that decent. Another time he drove twenty-two miles in freezing fog to pay somebody back when I had overcharged them for eggs. But that was when we were in the middle of a quarrel, so he could simply have been scoring a point.

Nor did I involve the children, for the same reason. Throughout the spring I worked away during school hours, accompanied only by Abbie, who was three and who couldn't sneak on me. She carried the trowel on our daily pilgrimage to the wood, which I now considered ours, its every clump of couch grass dear to me. When boxes arrived from obscure plant nurseries I told Edwin that I was really getting to grips with the garden. He was delighted, of course. He never noticed the lack of progress there; he hardly ever went into the garden, he was too busy. In fact he didn't know anything about plants; he just had strong opinions about them in a vague sort of way. He was like that with the children.

While he battled against the bureaucrats – the Stop the Road campaign wasn't getting anywhere – I glowed, my cheeks grew roses, my fingernails were crammed with mud. I felt as heavy as a fruit with my secret; I hadn't felt so happy since I was pregnant.

I was also becoming something of an expert. For instance, on *potamogeton densus* and *riccia flutans*. Latin names to you, but essential aquatic oxygenators to me. I bought them at my local garden centre, which had an Ornamental Pond section, and carried them to the wood in plastic bags. I had dug out the pond, and turfed its sides.

Then there was *triturus cristatus*, or perhaps *cristati* because there were four of them, courtesy of Mabel. Perhaps you don't know what this is. It is the Great Crested Newt. The male has a silver streak on the tail, and at breeding time develops a high, crinkled crest and a bright orange belly. The female, without crest but with a skin flap above and below the tail, is 16.5cm long overall, slightly longer than the male. *I* was feeling slightly longer than the male; more vigorous and powerful.

For good measure, and why not, Abbie and I planted some surprising plants in the wood too, garden plants, and some blue Himalayan poppies. I had to use my Barclaycard for most of this, the whole operation was costing a fortune. And then there was my *coup de grâce*, the orchids. We planted the Lady's Slipper (*cypripedium calceolus*), the Lizard and the Bird's Nest (*neottia nidusavis*), all extremely rare, and purchased from a small nursery in Suffolk whose address I had found in the back of *Amateur Gardener*. I cut off all the labels, of course, I'm not a complete fool, I even went to university once. I planted them tenderly in the patches I had cleared amongst the brambles. Above us the birds sang, and the watery spring sunshine gleamed on the ivy which, lush as leather, trousered the trees. I even knew the trees' names now.

In all those weeks Edwin never visited the wood. He never had time. In the country people never have time to do things like that, unless someone comes to lunch. It's like living in London and never visiting the Tate Gallery unless some American friends arrive. Edwin was busy doing all the things that people who live in the country really do, like driving twenty miles to collect the repaired lawnmower, and then doing it all over again because the lawnmower still doesn't work. Like driving thirty miles to find some matching tiles for our roof, and discovering that the place has been turned into a Bejams. So he never knew.

They didn't build the ring road past us; they're building it through the riding stables. This is because our wood has been designated a site of Outstanding Scientific Interest. They've put up a proper wooden fence, and a sign. They are even thinking of building a car park. And instead of thundering pantechnicons we've now got thundering Renaults full of newt-watchers.

It's August Bank Holiday today and people have come from all over, it's been really interesting. They knock on our door, and ask the way, and admire our cottage – botanists in particular are very polite. We're doing a brisk trade in eggs, too. Ours are guaranteed salmonella-free because the hens are fed on my organic bread, which is so disgusting we are always throwing it away. Sometimes the people even leave their children here, to play with mine, while they tramp across the field to inspect the orchids. Danny, that's my eldest, has even started saying things like 'mega-crucial'. Now we have our own traffic jams I don't miss Camden Town at all.

70

What Edwin feels about this is best described as mixed. Still, his furniture business is booming because it's only two miles away and even he is materialistic enough to put up a notice, with a tasteful, sepia photograph and a map, pointing them in the right direction. And so much has happened during the day that we don't have to talk about his mother anymore.

This morning I decided to start doing teas. I'll buy Old-Style Spiced Buns at Marks & Spencer and throw away the packets. I've learnt a lot this past year, you see, about the *real* country way of doing things.

Family Feelings

Five Linked Stories

Fool For Love

How do these things begin? What's the moment? For Esther, it was seeing the back of his neck – the sight of it, smooth and boyish. Brown hair curling against it as he bent over a parcel in the dispatch room. She had a sudden desire to lean towards him and smell it – the warm, biscuity smell of youth. Men of her age, mid-forties – various things were happening to their necks, none of them an improvement. To hers, too. And suddenly they had all bought glasses. The last time she had had dinner with her ex, one of their stilted, we're-still-friends dinners, when the menu had arrived they had both startled each other by producing a pair of spectacles. His were half-moon, professorial things that had aged him ten years but of course it was no longer her place to tell him so. They had talked, as always, about the children. A safe topic. Well, safeish.

Esther worked in an advertising agency. Owen was twenty-six. *Twenty-six.* He packed parcels downstairs with an old boy called Clarence who had been there forever. Esther started bringing down stuff herself, instead of leaving it in her Out tray. She sprang downstairs to the beat of Capital Radio. At home she shouted at her children to turn the blasted thing down but here in the dispatch room she was suddenly skittish. One Friday she wore her daughter's lurex top, glinting with silver, and Owen raised his eyebrows.

'You free lunchtime?' he asked. She nodded. 'Want to help me buy a Christmas present for me Mum?'

He pulled some sellotape; it hissed like indrawn breath. Her heart soared and sank. A date, yes! But did he just want the advice of a mature woman?

After two weeks chatting in the dispatch room it was thrillingly intimate, to step into the outside world. Traffic roared down Regent Street; above them, angels blew trumpets into the drizzle. They gave up on the present, it was too wet, and ate kebabs in a plasticky café. Owen was slender and pale; she had a shamefully maternal desire to fatten him up. Maybe he was just a substitute son to replace her real one who had gone to Goa in his Gap year and would soon be gone for ever.

She said: 'Toby, that's my son, he despises what I do, filling the world with consumer durables nobody needs. Huh, he can talk – you should see his bedroom!'

Owen gazed at her over his cappuccino. 'What about it?'

'Crammed with TVs and ghetto blasters and blooming consumer durables – ' She stopped. You couldn't complain about adolescents to somebody who was practically one himself. 'He's in Goa,' she said. 'They all travel. They're so blasé nowadays. Popping malaria pills and telling each other they'll rendevous in some Bengali flophouse. *See you in Beijing*, they say, *see you in Buenos Aires*.' She nearly said *in my young day we were lucky to go to Broadstairs* but she stopped.

Owen rolled a cigarette and grinned. 'You like dancing?' he asked.

And so it began, their affair. They went dancing in clubs which were so dark that nobody could see what an idiot she looked, clubs which pulsated to the jungle beat of her past. It had been so many years since she had fallen in love, since she had embarked on this adventure. Since she had mooned around in a dream, smiling at check-out girls. Since she had shaved her legs every single day. How exhausting it was, being attractive! She borrowed her daughter's clothes, picking her way like a carrion crow through the debris on Kate's bedroom floor. She spent hours in the bathroom, Kate rattling the door; she spent hours on the phone, Kate sighing loudly because none of her friends could get through. She yawned through work; like a student she never read newspapers and lost track of what was on the TV – she, supposedly a media person! Supposedly a mother, too. But one night she fell asleep at Owen's flat, the other side of London, and woke with a start at 7.30. She grabbed the phone.

'Time to get up!' she said to Kate. 'Time for school! Remember your homework!' She rolled back, sighing, into Owen's slim young arms. So much for motherhood.

Two weeks passed. Various small milestones had been surmounted, various *first times*. She had woken up with a disgusting stye in her eye and Owen still found her attractive. She had lent him £10 – he never had any money – and he had paid her back: see, he wasn't using her! He had seen her snarl with rage at another driver and hadn't been repulsed. They had not yet encountered true triumph or disaster and seen if they treated these two imposters just the same, but each minor incident shunted them further into intimacy. She felt alternately very old and ridiculously young. Certain things made her feel her age: the awful music he listened to, the way he asked her eagerly if she had actually seen Jimi Hendrix live. By having to explain so many things to him she realized how much the world had changed since the sixties, how nothing remained the same – nothing except perhaps Marmite. Lying in bed one Sunday morning, in his flat, and feeling guilty that she wasn't with her daughter, she told him a joke (ah, to have a new person to hear ones jokes!).

She said: 'There was this boy who was always late for

school. Finally the teacher made him stand in the corner, and not come out until he had answered a question right. It was a geography lesson and the teacher asked the class where the Rhodesian border was. The boy put up his hand. *I know where the Rhodesian boarder is*, he said. *He's in bed with me Mum, that's why I'm always late for school.'*

Owen asked: 'What's Rhodesia?'

'Oh, of course – it's Zimbabwe now.' So much to explain, but how delightful to explain it while running her finger along his smooth young buttock!

The only other problem – no, not problem, discrepency – was money. She lived in a house in Chiswick crammed with the consumer durables her son despised – even more so, it seemed, now he had arrived in Nepal and phoned her saying how spiritual it was to live unencumbered by material possessions, a phone call interrupted by Kate grabbing the receiver and yelling 'Mum's got a toyboy!'

Owen had never travelled. He lived in a bare, squatter-type room in Leytonstone. He didn't even have a TV because he couldn't afford the licence and even his cassette recorder was broken. He lived off the sort of food, like tinned pilchards, she thought nobody ate anymore except pensioners. Maybe the young did, but the only young she knew were her children's friends who ate *moules marinières* from Marks & Spencer because their parents were career people with large disposable incomes and no time to cook.

Owen came from a working-class family. His dream was to become a minicab driver, to be independent and work his own hours. The humbleness of this ambition humbled her. She thought of her own children, who had been given everything but who still complained, for adolescents have to complain about something.

The trouble was, Kate now had cause for complaint. She clomped about the house mulishly, in her great boots, slamming doors. She said her mother was never there, and there was never anything in the fridge. She said her lurex top had never been the same since her mother wore it. Esther smiled dreamily and said she would buy her another one.

'What shall I buy Owen for Christmas?'

'A teething ring.'

'Kate!'

'A potty.'

'Shut up! Just because I'm a woman! Your friend Paula's father's married someone half his age and nobody thinks *that's* odd.'

'You're so *embarrassing*,' said her daughter.

'You should be proud of me,' said Esther.

'Anyway, it's not fair.'

It was true. There was her daughter, aged seventeen, primed up and ready for romance. A thousand magazine articles had told her how to tone up her thighs and always use a condom. Products, some of which Esther herself promoted, promised to bring her love if only she rubbed them into her hair and painted them onto her lips. The bathroom was full of bottles and tubes, including an oatmeal face gel for which Esther had created the slogan *Face the Meusli*. It wasn't fair.

'Don't you like him?' Esther bleated. They were having a rare evening alone together.

'He's just using you.'

'Kate! Why are you all so cynical, you young people?'

'He must be. Why else would he want an old bat like you?'

'I'm not an old bat. I'm an experienced woman. He says girls his age are too aggressive.' She looked down at her daughter's feet. 'And wear such hideous boots.'

'He *is* using you.'

'When there's an age difference people always think that. An old man with a doting young starlet – they think it's a trade-off. But all love is an emotional trading transaction.'

Kate jerked her head towards the stairs. 'I know he's using you. I've just been into Toby's room.' She looked at her mother like a schoolmistress at an errant pupil. 'I've seen what's happening.'

Esther fell silent.

Ten days before Christmas, Toby came home. Esther stood at Heathrow Arrivals. She didn't recognize him until a voice said 'Hi, Mum.'

She jumped. Her son's skin was burnished caramel, his scarecrow hair bleached yellow. His body, when she hugged it, felt bony – wasted by subcontinental digestive disorders. She felt a rush of maternal love – the same rush she had felt when she had first seen Owen.

'How was the flight?' she asked.

'A baby screamed all the way from Dubai but it was OK. I meditated.'

'You? Meditated?'

He rummaged in his rucksack and gave her a book – *The Radiant Truth* by Swami Somebody. 'Once you reach Nirvana you feel so light.' He staggered, loading his rucksack onto his back. 'So free. You, like, shed the material world.' He pointed to a page. '*Detachment is the deliberate renunciation of desire for objects seen or heard.*' He looked around. 'Why're we going this way?'

'We're taking the tube.'

'What's happened to the car?'

'I'll tell you later,' she said.

Back home, her son went into his bedroom and dumped his rucksack on the floor. He took out a framed picture and put it beside the bed. It showed a fat Buddha, his eyes closed. Toby took out two joss-stick holders and placed them on either side, like an altar. Then he stopped, and looked around.

'Where's my ghetto blaster?' he asked. 'Hey, where's my TV?'

Esther tore open his packet of joss-sticks. 'Shall I light one?' she asked.

'Mum, where are they?'

Kate appeared in the doorway. 'She's given them to her toyboy.'

'*What*?'

'Lent them,' corrected Esther, striking a match. 'You don't mind, do you?'

'And she's lent him your walkman and your calculator and —'

'*Mum*!' bellowed Toby.

'Darling, they're just material possessions.' Dreamily, she watched the smoke unfurl from the joss-stick. 'Owen needs them more. I'm just helping you on the path to Nirvana.'

Kate fingered the row of studs in her ear. She looked at her mother. 'You told him about the car yet?' she asked.

Esther knew she was a fool – a fool for love. She knew this, but what the hell. She that tooketh from her children with one hand, she giveth to her lover with the other. For her own son was already loosening himself from her, as he must. Toby drove, shaved, was capable of producing his own children. His address book was filling up with unfamiliar names and when she spoke to him he rocked on the balls of his feet like his father did, as if he was getting ready to run. Soon she would be left alone, so who could call her a fool? Not her son. Nor her ex, because it was no longer his place to do so.

'You've *what*?' Toby stared at her.

She put on her new reading glasses and opened his book. '*When non-covetousness is firmly rooted the yogi knows his past, present and future.*'

81

'But I'm meeting my mates tonight,' he said. 'Like, a reunion. I've got to have the car!'

She read: '*The journey to enlightenment is a long one –* '

'I've got to get to bloody Muswell Hill!'

'I'll call you a minicab,' she said.

Ten minutes later the doorbell rang. Toby looked out of the window into the wintry night. 'That's our car!'

Esther nodded and opened the door. 'Hi, Owen,' she said, and kissed him. 'Meet my son, Toby.' She propelled Toby down the step. 'Here's your driver. You can get to know each other on the way. And he won't charge you; it's on the house.'

The Use of Irony

She called Barnaby the Barnacle. He was her little half-brother and he clung to everything. He clung to her leg when she was trying to get to the lavatory, he clung to her calf when she was trying to do her homework. He unthreaded the laces to her boots and then he couldn't – or wouldn't – thread them back again. If he were the cat she would kick him off.

'Can't you take him, Dad?' she pleaded. 'I'm trying to work!'

'So am I!' he bellowed, pounding upstairs. Paula's father was a writer. He wrote books about a detective called Norman who suffered from clinical depression. In each book Norman grew gloomier. Her father was very fond of his detective but as yet Norman had failed to grip the public, sell in vast quantities or be turned into a TV series. Her father slammed his study door; he had a deadline. But then so did she.

Paula was trying to write an essay entitled 'The Use of Irony in *Cold Comfort Farm*'. She had to finish it by the end of term but she hadn't even started it yet. Home was so chaotic, that was why. The house was so small with Barnaby in it. Simone, her stepmother, was training to be a psychotherapist and she liked to have quality time with Barnaby when she got home. This meant that Barnaby didn't get to bed till late and spent the evenings screaming around the house pretending to be a fighter jet. He liked launching himself from the settee and landing on Paula's stomach. Wherever she spread out her notes, the cat sat on them. Then there was her father, padding around because he had writer's block, making himself cups of tea and engaging everyone in conversation but scuttling away the moment Barnaby approached. Finally there were her stepmother's women friends who were all going through personal crises. They hung around in the kitchen drinking wine and blocking Paula's route to the fridge. Why did adults always fill up the kitchen when they had a sitting room to sit in? It meant that Paula couldn't get to the Pecan Nut Crunch without her stepmother spotting her and thinking she had an eating disorder.

Simone was much younger than Paula's Dad – only thirty-two. She was beautiful in all the ways Paula wanted to be – like being thin, with masses of black hair that somehow looked sexy and wild, whereas Paula's just looked a mess. When she moved in she said she didn't want to be a stepmother type of person, she wanted to be Paula's friend, her confidante, just girls together. She said if ever Paula wanted to talk, she would be there. She said *talk* in a special way, a capital letters way, that filled Paula with unease and somehow made the walls of the house close in around her.

The trouble with Simone was that she was too understanding. She understood Paula's feelings about her mother, who had run away to Totnes with a man who made stained-glass windows. She understood about being plump because she said – unbelievably – that she too had once had a weight problem. She understood about being adolescent because she was still practically one herself, and besides, she had written a paper called 'Psychodrama and the Teenage Dynamic'. What she didn't understand was the main point of being seventeen, which was to be misunderstood.

'If only she was older,' Paula said to her friend Kate. 'I want her to be like a parent.'

'No parents are like parents anymore,' said Kate bitterly.

'Even the real ones. Mum borrowed my leggings last night and spilt effing red wine down them.'

'Your shiny ones from Camden Lock?'

Kate nodded. Her mother had fallen for a young bloke called Owen and was making a complete wally of herself. 'Last night they started dancing to Rod Stewart. Rod Stewart! The curtains were open, anyone could see! And swigging Becks from the bottle. Mum doesn't even *like* beer. It's so sad!'

Their similar predicament had drawn them closer. Paula, from her years of experience, described the humiliating early days of her father's relationship with Simone, when he had grown designer stubble because he thought it looked trendy but at his age just made him look like an alcoholic. Why couldn't they just grow old properly? Kate snorted. 'They behave like bloody teenagers. They'll be bringing home traffic cones next.' It was she and Paula who felt like the elderly ones, clucking and disapproving. Somehow there was no space for them; it was as if their parents were sucking out the oxygen of their own growing-up.

'There's no space at home,' said Paula. 'Simone wants to talk to me about boyfriends but I can't tell her I haven't got one. She'd say *do you want to talk about it?* Ugh!'

Kate said there was no space at home because Owen was always there, giggling with her mother or watching TV with his cowboy-booted feet on the coffee table. 'He's always staying over because she feels so guilty leaving me and staying with him. They take showers together in the morning! It's so pathetic!' It was worse now, apparently, because he had just left his job and become a minicab driver, using their car, and dropped in at odd times of the evening just when she was settling down to her homework.

It was ten days before Christmas. They were walking home from school. Along Chiswick High Street a mannequin Father Christmas beckoned them into the car wash. Despite his lopsided hood he looked wiser than their parents; his head nodded, as if he knew all the answers. Term ended soon and Paula still hadn't started her essay.

'Can't I come and work at your place?' she asked. 'At least your mother's boyfriend's grown up. At least he won't start bouncing on top of me.'

'Don't be too sure,' said Kate.

At least at Kate's house she would get some peace and quiet. Toby, Kate's brother, had just come back from India but he wouldn't be any trouble; he spent most of his time in his room smoking dope and reading *Viz*. Besides, Kate's house was bigger than hers and other people's fridges, like their bookcases, were always more interesting than ones own.

The next day, after school, she had a brainwave. Toby could be useful. 'Just dropping round to Toby's place,' she said casually. 'You know – Toby, Kate's brother. He's really nice.'

Her stepmother's eyes widened, luminously. Then she smiled. 'It's happened at last,' she said. 'I'm so glad.'

So Paula went round to Kate's house and, under the guise of having a boyfriend, started to tackle her essay. When she got home Simone smiled at her in a twinkling, us-girls type of way. 'Is he nice?' she asked. 'Do you want to talk about it?'

'I'm a bit tired,' said Paula, who had been struggling all evening with her participles.

There was a problem. Though it was liberating, to get out of the house, Paula found that she had only exchanged one set of distractions for another. The problem was Kate's mother and her toyboy. Owen was reasonably good-looking in a preeny, fancying-himself kind of way but his eyebrows met in the middle and *Just 17* said that showed he was not to be trusted. And his clothes! He wore, would you believe, a cowboy shirt, one of those sad things with bootlaces. No wonder he liked Rod Stewart. When he arrived at the door Kate's mother called down the stairs: 'Have him washed and sent up to my room!' Until recently she had been quite a dignified sort of person. When he wasn't nuzzling up to her he engaged the girls in conversation, presumably to ingratiate himself – what were their favourite bands, that sort of stuff.

However, it was even worse when he wasn't there. Kate's mum mooned around the house, playing soppy music, and then would knock on their door when they were trying to work and fling herself down on her daughter's bed.

'Don't ever fall in love,' she sighed, 'Oh God, I ache when he's here and I ache when he's not here, I feel such a fool. This morning, when I saw he'd opened the window in the bathroom I just gazed at the catch, thinking *his* hand had touched it, am I mad?'

'*I* opened the window in the bathroom,' said Kate. 'It was my hand.'

'I can't eat, I keep thinking how it can't last, how one day he'll have children with somebody else, somebody young like him. I can't work –'

Nor can I, thought Paula, gazing at her notes.

'I gaze at this poster campaign we're doing and all I can see is his face –'

'It's not love, what you've got,' said Kate. 'It's called limerance. I read about it in *Marie Claire*. It's a sort of intoxication, sort of madness, it lasts six months and helps you not get womb cancer.'

'I keep on thinking, is he using me? Because I've got a car, because I feed him up and look after him, because I'm taking him off on holiday after Christmas –'

'When?' demanded her daughter. 'Where?'

'Venice. When you're going skiing with your Dad.'

'You never told me!'

'I'm so old! Look at my wrinkles. Look at my neck, soon it's going to be like a turkey's, I'm getting so flabby. When I run down the street to catch the bus – '

'Yeah – because *he's* got the car – ' said Kate.

'When I run, I can feel the tops of my arms wobbling. He's so young! Maybe we've got nothing in common. He doesn't even know where Rhodesia is!'

There was a pause. 'Where is Rhodesia?' they asked.

When she had gone Paula said: 'You've got to get her out of the house. Tell her to stay over at his place – '

'She feels so guilty when she does that,' said Kate. 'Last time she phoned to wake me up and I didn't hear it and missed school – '

'Please! Tell her you don't mind if she stays with him, you don't mind if she *lives* with him, we can look after ourselves, go on! Your brother's here. We can have the whole house to ourselves!'

They went downstairs and began their campaign.

'It'll be so romantic,' Kate urged her mother, 'so sexy. You and Owen, alone in his little room. Just you and him. Breakfast in his sunlit kitchenette. You need time together, to get to know each other. It says so in *Cosmopolitan*.'

When people want to do something they don't need much persuading. Kate's mother agreed to stay more nights at her boyfriend's place. Paula went home, glowing with triumph. Three more days of term – at last she would get her essay done. Simone smiled at her as she came in the door.

'You look wonderful,' she said. 'How's it going? Do you want to talk about him?'

Paula sighed. 'When he opened the bathroom window I looked at the catch and thought: ooh, his hand's touched that.' She sighed. 'I ache when I'm with him and I ache when I'm not with him – '

Luckily she was interrupted by Barnaby shooting at her, rat-a-tat-tat, with his imaginary gun.

The trouble was, it didn't turn out as she expected. What does? You think you know your parents and suddenly they grow designer stubble. Or they start getting skittish and nicking your lipliner. You think you know your best friend and suddenly you realize that her motives were completely different from your own. How could you have misunderstood her so completely?

The moment her mother was out of the house Kate shouted to her brother: 'Get my phone book!'

Toby came pounding down the stairs, they started telephoning and within an hour the house was filled with their friends. 'While the cat's away . . .' laughed Kate.

They started rolling joints and cracking open cans of Heineken. Toby turned up the volume on the CD player. Paula tried to escape upstairs but Kate's bedroom was crammed with girls from school smoking Marlboros and giggling about who was getting off with who in the living room. Nobody noticed when Paula, clutching her notes, let herself out of the front door and went home.

Her house was quiet. Simone was out at her Inner Healing evening class. Her Dad lay snoring on the settee, Barnaby asleep on his stomach. Now Barnaby was unconscious he looked so sweet she wanted to wake him up. Ironic, she thought. Then she pulled out the Shorter Oxford Dictionary to look up the word.

She sat down at the kitchen table and leafed through the pages. '*Irony:*' it said: '*A contradictory outcome of events as if in mockery of the promise or fitness of things.*'

Suddenly she was filled with a deep peace. She uncapped her Pentel and started to write her essay.

Rent-a-Granny

Munro had been married three times and by now he had been accused of everything. Three fierce and articulate women – between them they had covered most of the ground; that mud-churned battlefield. According to his wives his failings included: drinking too much, not being supportive, not noticing when they had got their hair done, the usual selfishness, egocentricity, unresponsiveness, laughing at his own jokes, repeating his own jokes, leaving the lav seat up . . . just being a *man*.

Then there were his children's accusations. His eldest daughter from his first marriage, Tabitha, accused him of being in denial – or maybe of putting *her* in denial, it was usually one or the other. She was thirty-two and had been in analysis for years. She accused him of setting up an abuse pattern which seemed to stem from him not turning up once for her School Sports Day. He had never been allowed to forget it. In his opinion, when somebody reached thirty an amnesty should be declared; they should lay down their arms and say they were grown-up now and nothing was their parent's fault anymore.

Paula was his teenage daughter from his second marriage. In many ways she had been his loyal ally through rocky times, but even she accused him of smoking too much and foisting Barnaby on her.

Barnaby, his little son, accused him of being a wibbly-wobbly dumdum. Barnaby was only four and hadn't honed his arguments yet. Mostly he bounced up and down on Munro's balls and prodded him with his Sten gun –

simpler weaponry than the women used, but painful all the same.

At the moment, in fact, Barnaby was his main problem. It was the week after Christmas and Munro was trying to work. It was prime working time – that hibernating period between Christmas and New Year, cold and grey, London closed down, a city under a spell, and everyone away. Christmas itself had been exhausting as usual, its festive spotlight pitilessly illuminating the cracks and fissures of his personal life. But it was over now and he had a clear week to get on with his book.

Or so he thought. But then it turned out that Simone, his wife, was planning to spend the week attending a course. Held in some women's centre, it was one of her empowerment-type things called 'Freeing the Warrioress Within'. As if she didn't terrify him enough already. It always amazed him, how the fiercest women he knew went on courses that taught them how to be even more alarming. The timid ones, who might have needed it, never did.

Simone was only thirty-two, the age of his eldest daughter. She possessed the certainty of youth plus this new steeliness they seemed to be born with nowadays. How did young men deal with this current crop of women? It was exhausting enough when one was fifty-six, with a certain amount of experience under ones belt. A few years ago women were loud and demanding. Now it was much more insidious; they simply took it for granted that a bloke would be supportive of their work, of their parenting, be a new man and look after Barnaby.

Munro was a sociable chap, prone to padding around the house searching for somebody to talk to, welcoming interruptions because it gave him an excuse not to get on with his book. On his door he had pinned up a notice: *Please Disturb; Writer at Work.* But Barnaby's interruptions were of a different order. To be perfectly frank, he hadn't wanted to have another child, nappies, all that. He was getting too old for it. He had done it too often. But Simone had wanted a child and he had wanted to oblige her because it seemed so selfish otherwise. He loved his beautiful young wife. It was his third marriage and he had to make a go of it or else people would start thinking there was something wrong with him.

The first couple of days were all right. He roped in his reluctant daughter Paula to help, but then she went away to stay with her mother in Totnes. Barnaby went to a playgroup in the mornings, but by the time Munro had taken him there, come home and settled down to work it was time to pick him up again. How short the days were, and how long the hours of darkness! What could he *do* with him? He needed, desperately, to have some time alone with Norman.

Norman was his detective, the hero of his three latest books, a gloomy man who lived in a bedsitter and was prone to long interior monologues. Munro's publishers were getting worried about Norman; they said the plots kept getting held up by Norman's bitter broodings about women. Munro said they weren't bitter, they were profound. His publishers said the books weren't selling because thrillers should have a plot, that was why people read them, and that Munro's stories were getting more meandering with each book.

Munro slotted in a Postman Pat video. 'Postman Pat!' he called, cheerily, to Barnaby.

His son came charging into the living room and flung himself on the settee. Munro tried to sneak away. 'Watch it with me!' yelled his son, grabbing Munro's leg.

After ten minutes Barnaby closed his eyes. Munro tried to extricate himself again but Barnaby was too quick for him. He gripped his hair – or what was left of it. 'Watch this bit!'

Munro sat there, mute. If his eyes strayed from the

screen Barnaby sensed it, by radar, and jerked his head back. Trapped, Munro watched the little red van bounce over the green hills. Postman Pat had a plot. Things got delivered. What worried him was that he had started this book without any idea how it was going to end. The general gist was child-kidnapping – wishful thinking, no doubt – but he was simply hoping that if he went on writing, something would work itself out. He had always found stories difficult. In one of his maudlin moments, when he was thinking how much sooner he would die than Simone, he had said to her: 'I know what you must put on my tombstone: *A Plot At Last.*'

He tried to reassure himself by thinking of Raymond Chandler, who apparently got in such a muddle he couldn't work out who was supposed to be killing who. Raymond Chandler had done all right, hadn't he?

At two o'clock Tina, their cleaner, arrived. She had been coming to them for a couple of months and Munro liked her because she was the sort of woman they didn't make any more, at least amongst his acquaintance – a woman who dressed for men. She had dyed blonde hair, shiny red lipstick and, most cheering of all, a little gold chain around her ankle. His spirits always lifted when she tap-tapped into the kitchen and inspected herself in the glass of the microwave.

'Tina,' he said, 'I'm desperate. When you've finished, could I pay you for another hour to take Barnaby out?'

'Where?'

'Anywhere. Anywhere but here. Just an hour,' he wheedled.

She agreed. They would be back by six. Munro went upstairs and sat down at his computer. Norman was having trouble meeting his alimony payments; Munro could write this from the heart.

The problem was, an hour was so short. Munro's eyes strayed to his pile of stationery. He picked up a packet and read: *'The Ivy range of self-adhesive labels. For almost every need.'* Almost every need? What about hunger? Loneliness? Could you use self-adhesive labels for that? Could you use them for sticking Barnaby to the settee?

An hour seemed to have passed. It was six-fifteen and they hadn't returned. Munro went downstairs and poured himself a whisky. Simone would be back at six-thirty – they must be home before she arrived. Why? Why shouldn't she find out? What was wrong with paying one's cleaning lady to look after one's child?

Because it would be an admission of defeat, that he couldn't cope. That he couldn't even manage a few days of bonding with his son. That he would rather entrust Barnaby to a flighty young woman whose address they didn't even know. Simone would – oh God – want to *talk* about it. He looked at the leaflet for her course. *'During our workshops we learn to recognize the warrioress within, set her free and develop true empowerment.'* He wailed silently: she's empowered enough already! She frightens the life out of me!

The doorbell rang. It was Tina and Barnaby. His mouth was smeared red. As she ushered him in she said: 'Sorry. See, I had to get my legs waxed and it took ages. I bought him a lolly.'

'Er – what about tomorrow?'

'Can't.' She winked at him. 'I'm meeting somebody. Hence the wax.'

'So where's your husband then?'

'In Wokingham.' She smiled. 'In fact, if I don't come in next week, can I use you as an alibi?'

He stared at her. What was the world coming to? 'An alibi? Then I'll have to do my own bloody cleaning too!'

She giggled. He bundled Barnaby away to wipe the red stuff off his mouth. For some reason, it looked adulterous.

The next day Tina the cleaner rang. 'There's an old dear upstairs called Oonagh. She'll take your son.'

So that was how Munro rented a granny. Oonagh was the real thing – cosy, dumpy, grey-haired, looking as if she had forgotten what sex was like forty years ago. In fact, Munro realized with an unwelcome jolt, she was hardly older than him. Her own grandchildren were scattered across Britain and Canada; she missed them, and took to Barnaby on sight. 'What a duck!' she said.

He considered keeping it a secret from Simone but he had visions of his warrioress-wife spotting her son in the high street hand-in-hand with this elderly child abductor and giving chase. Besides, Barnaby was bound to spill the beans so he got in first. He decided to make a joke of it. 'Maybe I'll give up the writing and start a business called Rent-a-Gran,' he laughed. 'A sort of inter-generational introduction agency. It suits both sides, see. There's so few bona fide grannies left, most of them are having HRT and running their own companies. Look at your own Mum.' Simone's mother was the PR for a rock band and currently having an affair with the bass guitarist. Catch *her* crocheting beside the fire.

Simone poured boiling water on to her herb tea. 'So this woman's going to come three hours a day?'

'I need three hours, otherwise I can't get down to anything. Just till life begins again – his school and such.'

'Till life begins again – what a curious phrase. You mean life without our son.' She dredged out her teabag and flung it into the bin. 'Maybe I should cut this course and stay home myself.'

'Don't make me feel guilty!'

'No. *I* feel guilty.' She sighed. 'I chose to have him.'

Munro felt a steel clamp tightening around his temples. Oh, sticky labels, help me now! Help me stick together my marriage!

'I think we should talk this through,' she said.

'Not yet! Not till I've finished my book!'

He won – if anyone wins these things. Oonagh the surrogate granny ensconced herself downstairs and peace descended on the house. Oonagh wasn't empowered. No warrioress, she. Oonagh wasn't in denial; in fact she was completely unreconstructed.

'Little boys should only speak when they're spoken to,' she said, knitting needles clicking. Barnaby, stunned, sat obediently at her feet rewinding her wool.

Upstairs Munro gazed at his computer screen. Sounds drifted up, sounds from his own childhood. A past when grannies were grannies, roast on Sundays, a golden age. A world of security before women were empowered and cleaning ladies committed adultery. He closed his eyes; Proustianly, he could almost smell his father's pipe smoke.

Suddenly he pressed the delete button. *Delete document?* Yes. *Delete backup disk?* Yes. He fished out a piece of paper and wrote 'Chapter One.'

Forget the thriller. Real life was much more thrilling. Forget Norman the detective. Enter Norman the real man.

'Page One.' He would write a novel – a real novel, from the heart. A long, Joycean monologue, brooding and profound, bitter maybe, but funny too. It would be the story of his own life, a voyage into the interior. Forget police tactics; emotional tactics were much more interesting. A great, literary sponge, his novel would sop up the mess of his life and turn it into gold. And with mixed metaphors like that, who knows? It might even win the Booker Prize.

Munro picked up his Pentel and, just as his daughter did, two weeks earlier, he began to write.

Sex Objects

What was the national average – two-point-four times a week? No, that was children. How many times a week, max, after you had been married a couple of years like he had? Trouble was, you never knew what other people got up to, bedroom-wise, you never knew if you were, like, a normal sort of bloke. Nobody told the truth. In the pub, of course, they bragged. Take Robbie, their panel-beater. He claimed that last summer, on Paxos, he had done it minimum four times a day with a girl from Barclays Bank. But Robbie was a Glaswegian.

Desmond's wife Tina was a beautiful girl with strong appetites. He should be the luckiest man in the world. He *was*. He loved her vigour and her animal spirits. He loved the way she sashayed down the street, tossing her head when scaffolders whistled at her. She could whistle back through two fingers – something he had always admired and longed to be able to do himself. The energy of the woman! She cleaned people's houses, she waitressed for a catering company, she worked out at a gym, arriving home luminous with libido and pouncing on him like a panther. He must be the envy of every red-blooded male in London.

That was the problem. He knew he was lucky. That was what made it worse, his recent but unmistakable feelings of reluctance when it was time to go to bed. He knew the sounds so well – the rasp of the match as Tina lit the candle in the bedroom, the click of the stereo as she inserted her get-ourselves-in-the-mood cassette. This was currently a Motown compilation called *Night is the time for love*. He knew, by the length of time she was in the bathroom, that she was inserting her diaphragm. Before she got into bed she puff-puffed herself with perfume, ready for action. The stage was being set for his performance and of course he was willing but sometimes, just sometimes, a man had to get a good night's sleep. Or even catch up on his reading. Desmond had left school at sixteen and was trying to work his way through the classics, but for weeks now he had been stuck at page thirty-six of *Moby Dick*.

Then there were the weekends. Dozing, exhausted, in front of the TV, he would be woken by her nimble fingers unbuttoning his shirt. 'Let's have a quickie,' she would breathe into his ear. Only last week he had been making himself a cup of tea in the kitchen and found himself pinioned against the units. 'They can see us opposite!' he protested, indicating the window. But she just wiggled her fingers over his shoulder. 'Hi there!' she called. He went to pull down the blind and knocked over the geranium pot on the window ledge, scattering earth on the floor, but even that didn't deter her. The next day he had had a throbbing pain in his lower spine, from where it had been pressed against the fridge door.

Sunday mornings were the other time. Waking drowsily, he would hear her purposefully brushing her teeth in the bathroom. This meant that when she climbed back into bed she could kiss him properly – in her opinion it was only in films that people made love in the mornings with their mouths all frowsty. So then he would have to get up and brush his teeth too, and bang went his lie-in.

Putting it this way sounded unromantic but sometimes, to be perfectly honest, this was how he felt. His wife was becoming so impersonal; it seemed as if she were reading a manual over his shoulder. Sometimes he felt he was simply part of her work-out routine, a piece of gym equipment she was using to shape up her thighs and flatten her stomach muscles. He felt *used*.

Desmond worked at a garage called Chiswick Lane Autos. It was the week after Christmas, a busy period due to the number of silly buggers drinking and driving on the icy roads. Two major prangs were towed in on the Wednesday, a Mazda and an Escort GTI. He worked hard all day. When he got home Tina snuggled up and put his hand on her shin.

'Go on, feel!' she said. 'I've just had them waxed.'

'Give us a moment,' he said, slumping on to the settee.

'Don't then. Some people'd give their right arm to feel my legs.'

He stroked her bare skin with one hand, and picked up the mail. Amongst it was a brown paper package addressed to Mr Murphy, who lived in the maisonette next door. The paper was torn; a video cassette poked out. Tina grabbed it and wriggled it out of the parcel.

'The dirty bugger!' she giggled. 'I knew he was funny! The way he looks at me when I take out the rubbish!' She held up the video. He glimpsed the word *Lovers* and *Adults Only*. She lunged towards the TV. 'Come on, let's put it on!'

'We can't,' he said.

'Why not?'

'It's not ours.'

'Des!'

How could he explain to his wife that the thought of watching a pornographic video with her filled him with exhaustion? More than that – with a sort of cosmic despair? He got up. 'I'm going to make a cup of tea.'

'Typical!' she said, and added ominously: 'Some people I know would jump at the chance.'

He went into their little kitchen and gazed at the units. He suddenly felt lonely. What's it all about? he asked himself. Any of it?

He took the next day off to visit his mother in Wokingham

– his yearly Christmas duty. Tina wasn't coming; she said his mother was boring. His mother probably *was* boring for all he knew, but he knew her too well to use those sort of words and was obscurely disappointed that Tina did.

He said goodbye to his wife, who was plucking her eyebrows in the bathroom. She was humming. After their spat last night she seemed surprisingly cheerful.

He took the video with him. Just as he was poised outside Mr Murphy's letterbox, about to post it through, he heard footsteps and sprang back. Mr Murphy came out. 'Morning,' Des mumbled, and retreated to the car. He couldn't possibly let Mr Murphy know that *he* knew; he would post it back later, when the coast was clear.

When he got back that evening Tina was in the bath, humming again. 'You been in there all day?' he joked, peering around the door.

She jumped; the water sloshed. Then she shook her head. 'Been working flat out all afternoon, at Mrs Whatsits and then at that other place, you know, took hours. I'm totally shagged out.' And she slid under the foam.

The next morning he was under the bonnet of a Citroen CX when he heard a rattling, grinding sound. A car drew up in the forecourt and shuddered to a stop. It was a badly-damaged Volkswagen Passat; its side panel was caved in, part of the bonnet as well, and two of its windows were shattered. He recognized the vehicle – he had recently MOT'd it – and its driver, Mrs Wakeman. She had been coming here for years.

She climbed out. She looked pale; when she gave him the keys her hand trembled.

'You OK?' he asked, wiping his fingers on a rag. 'You just done this?'

'Not me,' she said. 'My boyfriend. He crashed it last night. *Ex-boyfriend.*' Suddenly she burst into tears.

Desmond sat her down in the office and passed her some kitchen roll. 'You mean he's dead?'

Mrs Wakeman shook her head. 'Wish he was.' She blew her nose. 'Oh, I could *kill* him! He's just been using me. Oh, I'm such a fool!'

'Want a cup of tea?'

'He was using my car for minicab work. I lent it to him, my children've had to stand freezing at bus stops, how could I have been so besotted? It's called limerance.'

'What?'

'A sort of madness. My daughter read about it in *Marie Claire*. My own children are wiser than I am! You got kids?'

He shook his head. Tina didn't want them yet, she didn't want to get stretch marks.

'There was a girl with him, you see,' said Mrs Wakeman. 'Sitting in the front seat.'

'Was she hurt?'

She shook her head. 'But she was in the front seat, don't you see? She wasn't a paying bloody passenger, she wasn't sitting in the back. She was a *girlfriend*. Anyway, he confessed.' She started sobbing again. 'I'm sorry. I shouldn't be telling you all this, but everybody else is going to say *I told you so.*'

He looked through the window, at the car. 'You contacted your insurance company? Looks like a write-off to me.'

'The whole thing's a write-off,' she said. 'We had nothing in common but I fooled myself into thinking we had. You meet somebody, you lust after their body, and from then onwards you make yourself believe you're soul-mates, you try to mould them into being what you want, you sort of re-invent them for yourself and then, once the scales fall from your eyes, you realize you've invented somebody who doesn't exist, that it's all self-delusion. I should know. I work in advertising.' She wiped her eyes. 'Are you in love?'

He poured water onto the teabags. 'Well, I'm married.'
She laughed, shakily. 'That's no answer.'
'Sugar?'
She shook her head. Rummaging inside her handbag, she pulled out a video. 'You don't want two tickets to Venice, do you?' She put the video on the desk and pulled out her cigarettes. 'I'm supposed to be going there with him next week. That's the video from the travel agents. We were going to watch it together tonight.' She offered him a cigarette. 'Don't you want to go to Venice? It'd be so romantic.'

'Can't,' he said. 'We're off to Florida next month.'

'Gosh. Doesn't everybody get around nowadays!' He knew what she meant – by *everyone* she meant *even garage mechanics*. She blushed. 'I mean, my son's friends,' she jabbered, 'they're always munching malaria tablets and whizzing off to Togoland. *See you in Guatamala!* they say. In my day we were lucky to get a week in Bognor Regis.'

'It's a different place now, the world,' he said. Then he added, surprising himself: 'Like, it used to be women who were sex objects. Now it's men.'

She smiled. 'Maybe that's what Owen felt. My boyfriend – ex. Sometimes I felt I was banging on a closed door, trying to get through. More and more desperate.' They paused for a moment. From the workshop came the *thwack-thwack* of Robbie, panel-beating. 'Still, it was fun while it lasted,' she said.

When she left Desmond felt strangely stirred. He thought of Tina, and their first holiday together in Portugal. How the sight of her tenderly-peeling shoulders had brought tears to his eyes. Why didn't he tell her how much she moved him? 'You never talk!' Tina said, accusingly. Was that what she had been doing, these past few months – banging away at him to get his attention?

He packed up early, at five. As he got into his car he

had a strong sensation of danger – so strong that it blocked his throat. Those baths, that leg-waxing – how could he be such a fool? He thought: I've got to do something now, before it's too late.

When Tina arrived home he led her to the settee. He turned off the lights and lit a candle.

'What's all this in aid of?' she asked.

He passed her a glass of wine and slotted in the video. He pressed *play* and sat down beside his wife. 'Let's feel those shins,' he murmured.

'I've got my tights on.'

She lifted up her bottom and he pulled them off. 'Mmm, nice and smooth,' he whispered, stroking her leg.

She pointed at the TV and laughed. 'So we're going to watch it?'

He nodded. 'It's called *A Place for Lovers*.'

The video came on. Sunlight shone on a row of gondolas, bobbing on the water. A voice said caressingly: *'Let us explore together the most romantic city on earth, a city for lovers . . .'*

'This is it?' she asked, surprised.

'Time has etched its mark on her face but it can never erase her ageless beauty . . .' said the commentator.

He stared at the TV. 'I brought home the wrong video,' he said. 'This is a thing about Venice.'

'Let us stroll across St Marks Square, bustling and cosmopolitan, and be serenaded by the plangent notes of a violin . . .'

She paused. Then she snuggled up against him. 'Oh well, never mind,' she said. 'This is a lot more romantic.'

And, as it turned out, it was.

I Don't Want to Know

Lara sat at the window, gazing at the cows, and wondered whether to go to her ex-husband's party. She had always been a creature of impulse. It was on impulse that she had run away from him in the first place, eight years ago. She wasn't used to weighing up the pros and cons – should she go, shouldn't she? – but it was New Year's Eve and that made it significant, particularly now Jupiter was in conjunction with Saturn.

Lara was a jeweller. She lived in Totnes with a man called Flange. His real name was Gilbert but only his intimates knew that and he didn't have many of those. None, in fact. Flange was a solitary, bearded man who made stained-glass windows. He didn't believe in New Year's Eve. He said that a truly spiritual person should treat every day as a new year. And he certainly didn't believe in parties.

Outside it had started to rain. The drops tattoo'ed on the corrugated iron of the outhouse. Within it Flange would be working in his customary silence.

Lara jumped up and looked at the timetable. There was a train to London at eleven-thirty.

'You've invited Mum?' Paula stared at her father.

The wine for the party had arrived. Munro was uncorking a bottle, purely for tasting purposes. 'I feel expansive,' he said. 'Did we buy any Twiglets?'

'She'll never come all this way anyway.'

'Why not?' he said. 'She might be curious.'

'Curious? Mum?'

'I know your mother's not overly interested in others, but even *she* might want to see if success has spoilt me.' He smiled smugly. 'Has it?'

'Yes,' said his daughter. 'If you play that video of yourself on *The Late Show* one more time I'll scream.'

Munro's novel had just been published to rave reviews. Strange to think that a year ago he had been gloomily struggling with a tinpot detective story. As he had told the *Independent*, his novel had come to him in a burst of inspiration and he had written it in three months flat. Now he was the darling of the literati, some of whom were coming to his party tonight. 'Shall I leave some copies of my book around, just casually?'

'No!' said his daughter.

'Wonder if your Mum recognizes herself in it.'

'She probably hasn't read it.'

He nodded. 'In Totnes they only read Tarot cards, don't they. Promise to deal with her if she gets embarrassing.'

'Dad, I've told you! I won't be here. I'm babysitting. It's triple-rate on New Year's Eve.'

Motherhood had changed Tina. Desmond's feisty young wife had been transformed overnight into a demure, contented – well, *mother*. Her face, innocent of make-up, looked bare and vulnerable. Once the life and soul of the party, she now stayed at home reading baby magazines and nursing their three-month-old son Bruce. When Des said 'It's New Year's Eve, I'm taking you up West,' she had stared at him as if he'd suggested a trip to the moon.

'We can't leave Bruce!'

'We'll get a babysitter.' He laughed. 'Seems funny, *me* having to persuade *you* to come out for a night on the tiles.'

She burped Bruce and laid him in his carry-cot. They gazed at him. It was hot in their little maisonette; Tina was terrified their baby might catch a chill. Bruce's carrot-coloured hair was plastered to his forehead.

Desmond had dark-brown hair and Tina's, now the blonde had grown out, was revealed as mouse. When their redheaded son was born Des had been startled. For a mad moment he had thought that all babies were born redhaired, like rabbits were born blind. Tina had said nothing. When a few weeks had passed and the hair remained red he had said it must be inherited from his great-aunty Dottie, who he had heard was definitely gingery on top. That must be the explanation. Tina had nodded wordlessly. The next day she had bought Des a beautiful leather jacket. 'What's all this about?' he had asked. She hadn't replied.

They got a babysitter – Paula, the daughter of one of Tina's old employers. At eight o'clock a minicab arrived to take them to Leicester Square where they were going to have an Italian meal. The driver, a young bloke in a cowboy shirt, asked if they liked country and western music and slotted in a cassette.

'... *your cheatin' heart*' crooned a man, '... *I been a fool ... to trust you ...*'

Des lit a cigarette and gazed out of the window.

Munro's party was in full swing. Barnaby, his little son, barged through the crowd and spilt Ribena down the leggings of the *Guardian*'s fiction critic. Munro mopped her up. 'Thank God you've already written your review,' he laughed. He had a growing suspicion that he was drunk; he had a sudden, clear memory of telling the same story twice. No, three times.

He looked across at his ex-wife, Lara. He hadn't seen her for years. She was ageing surprisingly well in a hippyish, patchouli sort of way. She was gazing fixedly at a woman called Esther, the mother of one of his daughter's friends. A lifetime ago, when he'd first met Lara, he hadn't realized why she had gazed at him so intensely; it was because she was too vain to wear her glasses. He had thought, erroneously as it turned out, that she was actually interested in what he was saying.

The minicab was driving through Hammersmith. A car slewed across the road in front of them. Their driver slammed on his brakes.

'Dickhead!' he shouted. He turned to them in the mirror. 'A year ago some drunken berk wrote off my car. Well, not *my* car. Side caved in. Girl I was with, one more inch and she'd've been dead.'

Desmond gripped his wife's hand. He thought of chance, of a few inches, of the fragility of life as the year rolled on its axis. The music crooned as they drove up Knightsbridge.

'... *all you do is tell me lies* ...'

'Isn't life amazing,' said Des to his wife. 'Like, pot luck. Like, if someone had pulled out a different raffle ticket I wouldn't have won that holiday in Portugal, I wouldn't have fallen in love with you, there wouldn't be a baby lying in his carry-cot –'

'Des –' she said.

He stopped her mouth with his finger. 'I just mean – accidents can happen. Or not happen. Either way it's, like, out of our hands.' He lifted up the champagne bottle. 'After dinner we'll take this to Trafalgar Square.'

Esther was still talking to Lara. She had to shout over the noise of the party. 'I used to work in advertising but I've just given it up. You see, this time last year I went to Venice with a woman friend and suddenly felt this lump. I thought – typical! I'm staying in the most romantic city in the world and I have to feel my own breasts! Anyway, they took the lump out and it was benign but the whole thing shook me up, shook up my priorities, and advertising seemed ... so trivial somehow ... and I'd made some disastrous mistakes in my personal life ...'

Lara, gazing at her, suddenly had a vision of Flange. He would be standing in the corner looking mutinous, itching to leave. He would be gazing at all these people and thinking *chatter-chatter, yackety-yack, what fools they look.* Lara gazed at the party guests and thought they looked a lot more interesting than the woman who ran the post office and why did it always rain in the country? Then she thought, with blinding clarity: Flange is boring. I'm bored to tears.

Esther was saying: 'What I really want to do is sell up and move to the country.' She gestured around. 'I'm tired of all this yackety-yackety media gossip. I want to move somewhere quiet and do my own thing ... painting ...'

'Jewellery,' said Lara automatically.

' ... jewellery. That'd be so creative. Funny they call *advertising* creative ... huh ...' She sighed. 'I know what *my* New Year Resolution's going to be. Move to the country and change my life.'

'I know what mine's going to be, too' said Lara. She moved away. 'Just going to find my daughter.'

Paula was looking after four babies. Once the word had got around, several neighbouring couples had grabbed at the chance of leaving their infants with her and going out to celebrate. She sat in Tina's lounge, the TV on low, surrounded by carry-cots. Their inmates slumbered. She had never liked New Year's Eve parties; it was so embarrassing, being kissed by people she had never seen before. That the event should be significant, and never was, made it worse. She worked out how much money she was earning and felt at peace.

At ten to twelve the doorbell rang. Her mother stood there, clutching a bottle of champagne.

'I pinched this from the party,' she said. 'I had to see the new year in with my daughter.'

The doorbell had woken up two of the babies; they started to cry. 'Now look what you've done' said Paula.

'Goodness, a crèche!' Her mother lifted up a yelling baby and vaguely joggled it up and down. 'Listen, I've made a New Year's Resolution. I'm sure it's in my stars. I've been thinking about you so much, my pet. I'm going to move back into London and be with you, where I belong. Mother and daughter together.'

'It's a bit late for that,' said Paula. 'I'm eighteen. I've finished school, remember? I'm going to Thailand next month. Oh hell!' The two babies had woken up the other two. They struggled to a sitting position in their carry-cots, whimpering, limbering themselves up to scream. Her mother was trying to uncork the champagne bottle with one hand. Suddenly furious, Paula pointed to the babies. 'How can you talk about mother and daughter! These parents have only left their kids for one night. *You* left *me* for eight years!'

'Darling, don't be so unforgiving!'

Paula hoisted a baby onto her hip. She went into the kitchen to heat up some milk. Her mother followed.

'Why did you leave me?' Paula demanded. 'You've never told me. I want to know.'

'Oh, it's a long story. Your father . . .'

Her voice was drowned by yells. 'Quick, take this bottle!' said Paula.

Back in the lounge the noise was deafening. Paula only caught a few words. ' . . . your father . . . selfish . . . unresponsive . . . no idea of my needs . . .' her mother raised her voice over the din. 'Then he started drinking . . .'

'Pass me that bottle!' yelled Paula, 'and that dummy!'

' . . . he was like a *child* . . .'

'Pick that one up! Can't you even change a nappy?'

The noise grew louder. Suddenly Paula looked at her

watch. Gripping a baby, she lunged to the TV and turned up the volume. Big Ben started striking. The screen showed Trafalgar Square; the crowd roared.

'SHUT UP!' Paula yelled – to the babies, to her mother. In the sudden silence she grabbed the champagne bottle and took a swig. 'I don't want to hear,' she said. 'I *can't* hear.' She passed the bottle to her mother. 'Happy New Year anyway,' she said.

It was twelve-thirty. Des and Tina sat in a taxi, travelling home. Their throats were sore from shouting greetings to complete strangers. For one magical moment, at midnight, Des had felt part of a huge family thousands strong. His own seemed so small, and besides Tina thought they were boring. Problem was, you couldn't choose your own parents, just as they couldn't choose you. Easier with strangers.

'Hope Bruce is OK,' Tina said.

'Don't worry. I'm sure he's fine.'

Tina picked a streamer off her coat. 'Des,' she said. 'There's something I've got to tell you. About Bruce.' She paused. 'A year ago –'

He put his hand to her mouth. 'Don't,' he said. 'Honestly, truly – I don't want to know.'

For the rest of the journey they didn't speak. When they arrived home, Tina had torn the streamer into bits. They lay scattered on her lap and fell off when she got up. When Des put the key into the lock, she nuzzled his neck.

In the lounge the TV burbled on, unwatched. The babies lay asleep in their carry-cots. On the settee slumbered their babysitter and an unknown, messy-looking woman wearing a lot of jewellery.

Des inspected the carry-cots, one by one. 'Which one's Bruce?' he joked, gazing down at the babies. He smiled at his wife. 'Hey, does it really matter?'

Tina held his gaze for a moment. 'They've left some

champagne,' she said finally, picking up the bottle. She fetched two glasses.

Des leant over Bruce's carry-cot. He planted a kiss on the baby's treacherous red hair. He whispered: 'Happy New Year to you too, mate.'

A Pedicure
in Florence

Be honest. Look into your heart. Do you prefer to get a postcard saying 'Having a wonderful time', or one saying 'Holiday a total disaster, wish we could come home'?

Helen, shamefully, felt a small rush of pleasure from other people's misfortunes. Perhaps she wasn't very nice at all; perhaps that was why Alan had divorced her. But then holidays with Alan had always been a strain; to compare them with other's non-successes was some small consolation, she supposed. Events conspired to irritate him – her map-reading, the children's bleary refusal to get up early and sieze the day, the presence of other British people in some remote and inaccessible location where he thought himself and his family alone and speaking the language like natives. She always remembered his bellow of pain when, staying the night in a chai house in the middle of the Hindu Kush, he had opened the visitor's book and found the names of Denise and Donald Waterman, the couple who lived opposite them in Ealing.

Such a strain, keeping him happy, silently urging the children to ask enquiring questions about Romanesque architecture rather than moaning that their walkman batteries had run out. But all that was over now; she was a single woman again. After twenty-two years she and Alan had parted. Mysteriously, marriage itself seemed to have been the *coup de grâce*. They had met in that long-lost golden age when everyone was hanging loose, hanging out, whatever they all did then. After seventeen years of living together and bringing up a family their increasingly

115

mutinous children had rebelled. 'We keep on having to explain to people!' they moaned. Finally, they delivered their own *coup de grâce*. 'It's so *seventies*, not being married.'

That had done it. Stung, she and Alan had gone to a register office and got married. Things had started disintegrating and within four years they were divorced.

Alan-less, the summer holidays approached. Welling up beneath her sense of panic and failure she was aware of an exhilarating new feeling – freedom. The children were almost grown-up; she was forty-four. She could go anywhere; do anything. She would do what she had always wanted to do: rent a house in Italy and not do anything cultural. She would swim and sunbathe and drink litres of red wine. She wouldn't visit any museums and churches at all – not unless she felt like it. Alan, laden with guide books, had always insisted they did these things thoroughly; he could even pronounce 'Ghirlandaio'.

She went with her friend Xandra, a cheerful, accommodating woman who was also man-less, though a veteran of two marriages and a recent disastrous liaison with a young motorbike messenger who worked at her courier firm. Helen was fond of Xandra, but the real basis of their bond was their two daughters, who were best friends at school and the only ones of their various children who had condescended to come on holiday with them.

'Four women in Italy!' chortled Xandra, snorting smoke through her nostrils. 'Two young, two old – three thin and one – ' prodding herself ' – fat. We're going to have a ball! They won't know what's hit them.' She laughed her laugh that sounded like dried beans rattling in a glass jar.

It started off all right. 'How romantic!' Helen cried as they drove up a gravel track. It climbed miles up a hillside above Perugia. The undercarriage scraped over a rock; they laughed. How grateful she was that Alan wasn't here to wince at the scraping noise, to hear the girls' complaints that it was miles from anywhere, to have heard Xandra's ribald and explicit assessment of the local talent lounging outside the village shop – or, as she put it, resting on their zimmer frames.

The house stood at the top of the hill – a handsome stone building complete with pool and a wonderful view. 'Look at the wonderful view!' cried Helen. The German couple who owned it lived in an apartment on the ground floor. The man, Hans, a bronzed, overweight bull in tiny trunks, was fiddling with the filter in the swimming pool.

'They *live* here?' hissed Annie, Helen's daughter. 'How am I going to take my top off?'

'Look at the swallows!' cried Helen. 'Look at the flowers! Oh look – a darling little lizard!'

They had forgotten to buy bread so Helen drove back down the gravel track to the village. It took twenty minutes and just as she arrived she saw the shutter crash down on the shop. She banged on it and after a moment an old woman with a flourishing moustache appeared and jabbered rapidly in Italian.

'*Aperto? Aperto?*' asked Helen. An old retainer sitting outside the bar held up four fingers. Watched by the row of geriatrics, she climbed back into the car. Half of her thought: I'm glad Alan's not here; *we* don't mind. We'll eat biscuits. The other half thought: if only he were here, he would have remembered that the whole country closes down from one to four.

When she returned she heard girlish laughter and splashes. Her spirits rose until she saw that it was not their two daughters jumping into the pool; it was a small, coffee-coloured girl wearing water-wings. Annie and Abigail sat fully clothed on the terrace, looking mutinous and scratching their mosquito bites. Charcoal smudges on the concrete floor betrayed where they had been stubbing out their Marlboros.

'There's somebody else staying with the Germans!' they

hissed. 'An Australian woman called Binkie!' They pointed to the little girl. 'That's her daughter!'

Binkie turned out to be a talkative, pear-shaped woman who was blithely unaware of their territorial rights to the pool. Like many single parents of a single child, she devoted herself to her daughter's development, informing her at some length about her every move. Her daughter was called Mena and over the next couple of days they learnt to stiffen as Binkie approached the pool. 'Now Mena, Mummy's going to take you for a swim and then you can have an ice lolly and then we'll lie in the sun with these nice people . . .' Presuming anyone who was reading had to be bored she would look at their books. 'Oh, *The Age of Grief*, Helen, is that a sad book?'

'She's always *here*!' hissed the girls. 'She's always talking! She's so boring!'

Xandra gazed at the little girl, splashing in the pool. 'Looks like the only interesting thing she's ever done is sleep with a black guy.'

It seemed churlish to object to a small child playing in their pool – after all, like them, Binkie was a single mother. Helen's irritation sprang partly from her own suspicion that she herself was being petty. So she smiled sweetly – so sweetly that Binkie stopped asking if she could use the pool and ensconced herself on the best lounger, the only one with a mattress.

The other problem – no, not problem, they did *live* there – was the German couple. Hans was always at the poolside, fishing out insects with his net or fiddling with a complicated tangle of filters and hoses. The girls tried to find a secluded place to sunbathe but then his wife came out there to hang up her washing and ask them what they felt about the Royal family. The girls retreated to the house.

'Look, we're still white! We've got to get brown, to show our friends! They're sitting on our terrace. They're using our barbecue!'

'They did ask,' said Helen. 'They've got friends coming round tonight.'

'Why didn't you say no?'

'I couldn't.'

Trapped by their own cowardice, they cowered indoors. Helen thought: if Alan were here – if any man were here – he would have made our territorial rights politely clear at the beginning. Women are so feeble. We are trapped by our eagerness to be liked. That evening, to avoid their hosts, they forsook the terrace with its swallows and its wonderful views over the Umbrian hills and drove down to the village where they sat in the small, concrete bar. Lit by a strip of fly-bespattered neon it was a quiet place, its clientele the geriatric men who spent the rest of the day sitting outside the shop. One of them cleared his throat and spat into a handkerchief. The girls gazed at the pensioners and stubbed out the cigarettes their mothers no longer had the strength to stop them smoking.

'When I was your age,' said Helen, 'I went on holiday with my parents to Malta and the first night I went out with a waiter and got love bites all over my neck. For the next whole week I had to wear a scarf. My parents kept saying *aren't you hot? Why don't you take it off?*'

Annie snorted. 'Huh. The only things biting us are effing mosquitoes.'

Abigail looked around. 'None of this lot have got any teeth anyway.'

Xandra, chuckling, leafed through her phrase book. '*C'é defetto. Me lo potrebbe cambiare!*' She looked up. 'These are faulty. Can I have a replacement!'

It took them a week to admit, openly, that their holiday was a disaster. Abigail had constipation, then diarrhoea, and spent a great deal of time in the lavatory, which abutted the kitchen. To spare her embarrassment they kept away from the kitchen, the walls were so thin, and just darted in to grab some food. How small the place seemed, and how many of them in it! Annie wrote long letters to her friends bemoaning the lack of men and wishing she were home. Xandra's period was late and, terrified that she had been impregnated by her toyboy motorbike messenger, she drove down to the village to phone him up but couldn't get through. Her daughter, who had overheard this from the lavatory, emerged and snorted: 'You're not pregnant. You're getting the menopause.' At this Xandra burst into tears and drank a bottle of Chianti. At midnight she staggered into the bathroom and threw up. 'I must be pregnant!' she wailed.

Helen, to escape, tried to go for a walk but unlike Xandra the countryside proved impregnable. Walking down one gravel path she arrived at a rubbish dump and walking down the other she was stopped by a gate saying STRADA PRIVATA. Walking back to the house she reflected upon the illusions of liberty. Now she was here, how free seemed her life in London! In Ealing she could walk anywhere. Unchained from the domestic grind she could shop anytime, rather than be in thrall to the siesta. Best of all, she had the personal liberty of her own privacy and didn't have to wait, behind a window, for the moment to dart out to the pool, and spend the rest of her time trying to find a tin-opener or gazing at someone else's hideous furniture. Outside the German invasion was gathering pace and several more house-guests had arrived; they lay around the pool, grilling themselves. Xandra said: 'I feel like pricking them with a fork.'

Trapped in the house, Xandra and the two girls began to get on Helen's nerves. They still had a week to go. In desperation she finally suggested a cultural expedition. They drove to Arezzo to see the Piero della Francesca frescoes. Sweltering in the heat, they parked in a tow-away zone and hurried into the church with ten minutes to go before it closed. In the gloom they could just make out a wall covered with flapping plastic sheeting and a sign saying IN RESTAURO.

When they got back the girls flung themselves on their beds and said they had finished their books and what on earth were they going to do now? They lay there sulkily, counting their mosquito bites. Helen was gripped by the same panic. What *does* one do on holiday?

So when the girls, exasperated by the lack of local talent, said they were going to take a day trip to Florence, she felt secretly relieved.

'You're only seventeen!' Xandra protested.

Abigail snorted: 'At seventeen you got pregnant with Ben.'

'Exactly,' said her mother. 'That's what I'm worried about.'

But after a short tussle the teenagers won and at an unearthly hour – unearthly for the girls – they were dispatched onto the train for Florence.

Can you sense these things? As a mother, can you sense them? At seven o'clock Helen began to feel uneasy. Xandra was trying to get her out to the terrace for a drink before the Germans emerged from the house. 'If we're sitting there already, maybe they won't talk to us,' she whispered – they had taken to whispering. After a week the Germans, encouraged by the women's feebleness, had presumed their company was always welcome and engaged them in long conversations about the British parliamentary system when they were trying to read their books.

They carried out their wine, willing Binkie not to join them with the latest instalment of the saga of Mena's tummy upset. They drank, unmolested. The girls were due back at ten-ish; they were going to take a taxi from Perugia station.

'What'll I do?' wailed Xandra. 'I can't have another baby! I'm forty-three!'

Helen, gazing at the sinking sun, thought of the hot bonds of motherhood, how one was never free of it, not until one died. How when even a grown child was absent a terrible scenario played over and over in ones head; increasingly lurid, it ceased only with the child's return. How could one start again with all that?

At ten o'clock she said: 'Do you think they're all right?'

At a quarter past eleven Hans appeared. 'Phone for you!' he bellowed.

It was Annie. They had been robbed. 'We were sitting on these steps outside the whatsit, the Duomo,' she sobbed faintly, 'and these boys came up to us and we thought they were so nice . . .' Her voice broke. 'We've only got this phone card and it's running out . . .'

Helen, her bowels churning, shouted: 'Check into a hotel, one that takes Visa cards! Wait for us there!' The line went dead.

The next morning Helen and Xandra drove to Florence. The girls had phoned with the name of their hotel and by noon they had found it – a leprous-looking pensione up a side street near the railway station. At the reception desk a man jerked his head, indicating upstairs. A fan lifted and lowered his newspaper.

In Room 26 the curtains were closed. It was a narrow cell, smelling of last night's cigarettes. The girls, who had only just woken, lay in bed watching an Italian game show on TV. Around them lay scattered the empty contents of their minibar. 'We've lived off it,' said Annie, as Helen hugged her. 'There isn't room service and we missed breakfast.'

With some pride, Abigail pointed out the empties to her mother. 'Coke, Kronenbourg, Sanpellegrino Aranciata, J&B, Campari soda, a bag of peanuts and that funny liqueur even *you* don't drink.'

Xandra's face froze. She looked at them all and then

darted into the bathroom. Behind the closed door they heard a yelp.

'It's started!' she called. 'Blimey, my period's started!'

Helen pulled open the curtains; the sun blazed in. Suddenly they all burst out laughing. Strange, wasn't it? Imprisoned in their cell, they were filled with joy. Why? Because they had found their girls? Because they were alone, at last? Because when they were supposed to be enjoying their holiday they weren't, and now they weren't, they were? Helen felt an airy, shuddering sense of liberation. Freedom is a Visa card, she thought. Freedom is not being pregnant. Freedom is not being married, for it seemed suddenly very simple to be four females alone in this squalid room. Nobody to blame them, nobody to know. Nobody to chastise the girls for being bored, for being uncultural, for being robbed. To celebrate, they shared the last bottle – Asti Spumante, which the girls hadn't touched because they thought it was champagne and too expensive. See – despite their mulishness they were nice really.

Later they sat on the rim of a fountain and ate pieces of pizza in smeary paper napkins. Junk food for tourists, according to Alan, but Alan wasn't here. And after lunch Helen didn't visit the Uffizi or the Pitti Palace or the Santa Maria Novella. She stopped somebody and, using the phrase book, asked: *'Dove it piu vicino . . .* er, *istituto di bellezza?'*

Never in her life had she done this before. Never in her life had she had a pedicure. She went into a scruffy little beauty parlour and sat in an airless cubicle whilst a chain-smoking beautician clipped her toenails and pushed back her cuticles. The only culture she saw was a view of Venice on the heaped ashtray, and a scorched reproduction of Botticelli's *Birth of Venus* printed on the lampshade.

She gazed at her toenails, freshly-painted crimson. She smiled at the woman. *'Bene!'* she said. She thought: freedom is doing exactly what I've always wanted to do. For the first time since her divorce – no, since way back in her marriage – she felt truly grown-up.

And later that day she wrote postcards. 'Having a terrible time,' she wrote, 'robberies, stomach upsets, boring Germans.' She wrote that because happiness made her generous.

Summer Bedding

I was planting the summer bedding when he talked to me. I was bending over, rump in the air. I was planting white begonias, red geraniums and an edging of verbena – well, *I* didn't like the colour scheme either. I was working in St James's Park and Big Ben chimed in time with the thrust of my trowel. Being so near to Parliamentary decisions made me feel vigorous and participatory. It made significant the packed, cylindrical roots of the plants I inserted into their new home, the old earth. In the Commons they were debating some law about press intrusion and I wondered if such a measure would ever take root.

Anyway, I straightened up and saw this trim, neat man. Grey beard; grey silk suit. Dapper. I wiped my hands on my dungarees. He asked me where he could get a cup of tea and I told him. 'I am so very obliged,' he said. So polite, but then he *was* foreign. He looked at me and sighed. 'Ah – Silvana Mangano.'

That dates him – dates me too. I was too young to have seen *Bitter Rice*. He said 'She stood like you stand – I thought, never have I seen such a magnificent creature.' He smiled. I felt the heat spreading into my face.

Later he came back. I was sitting on a bench drinking tisane from my thermos. Big Ben chimed five. He sat beside me and talked about movies. I said that when I came home I was so exhausted I could hardly switch on the TV. Note that I didn't mention my husband. This omission made me blush again. He lifted my arm. 'Your elbows,' he said, 'how charming they are!' He gazed at them. My skin

127

prickled. Nobody has ever noticed my elbows before. Gavin had never remarked on them. But then I had never said anything about Gavin's elbows either. In the silence a pelican flew up from the island, clattering and prehistoric.

He came back the next day. I was putting in the verbena – magenta, horrible colour. Somebody had left a *Sun* on the bench and I read that a scandal was brewing – a cabinet minister had been spotted canoodling with a comely young researcher. He sat down – his name was Bertrand – and said that in his country there was a *modus vivendi* for affairs of the heart, and to him the scandal was that it obscured the real scandals and removed able men from office. Didn't we all need romance in our lives?

He asked me to take a glass of wine with him. 'My hands! My clothes!' I cried.

'We will wash your hands,' he replied. 'As for the rest – you look the most radiant young woman in London. Others have to buy the colour of your cheeks in a little container.'

So that was how it began. That was how I, a married woman, became the mistress of a married man. My own summer bedding took place in a hotel room in Victoria. It happened during the lost hour after work. Down in the street, beyond the double-glazing, traffic flowed soundlessly. It was their rush hour but we took our time. My dungarees lay, guiltily empty, over a gilt chair; afterwards I washed myself with his complimentary shower gel.

I'm afraid he was Belgian – well, somebody has to be. He was also something to do with the European Commission but he didn't want to talk about that, it was too boring, and I certainly didn't want to hear. I never said a word about Gavin, either. His name, spoken aloud, would have felt too shocking. Bertrand and I existed in another dimension, disconnected, sealed in with its own adulterous air-conditioning. Is it always like this? I had never done it before, you see.

Back home Gavin would be hunched over his computer. For three years now I had been supporting us while he studied quantum mechanics – a subject that, like my liaison, existed on another inexplicable plane. We lived in a small flat in Kilburn – draughty, freezing in winter – and the real reason we didn't go to the cinema was that we had no money. We were saving up for central heating. Gavin and I were chums. Are chums. He calls my breasts 'boobs'. With Bertrand I became another creature – a woman. A real woman, the old-fashioned kind for whom doors are opened and whose breasts, not boobs, are worshipped. Who is given gifts.

Oh yes, he gave me those. And what gifts! The first was a bracelet with little jewels in it. Not my thing at all but that made it all the more arousing; I felt like a kept woman. There is something very sexy about being politically incorrect. A few weeks later he gave me a necklace with little blue stones in it. The next day I wore it under my tee-shirt while I heaved sacks of manure. That he was paying for my body made it delightfully precious; I bloomed for him. All these years I had been paying for a man and now a man was paying for me! These gifts were the jewelled equivalent of our love affair – utterly unlikely and disconnected to anything familiar. As old-fashioned as having a continental lover, as unlikely as the pelicans in St James's Park and almost as prehistoric. I told nobody, not even Janice who had trained with me at Wisley and who at the last count had slept with twenty-seven men. She would have found it hysterical. So I just wrapped the little boxes in brown paper and hid them under a loose floorboard in the bedroom. This hiding place seemed appropriately stagey, too – easing up the board made me feel as if I were acting in one of Bertrand's beloved Inspector Clouseau films.

So the summer passed. The cabinet minister resigned. Another scandal brewed; I read about it in a copy of the

Daily Express that somebody had left in a litter bin. An MP was spotted coming out of a gay video club; a week later he was found dead in his fume-filled Ford Granada. And in October Bertrand went back to Brussels.

He was charming to the end – courteous and regretful. I guessed that he had done this often before, but curiously enough I didn't mind. I felt like the last in a line of mistresses that stretched back not just through his life but back into history – kept women, *Mistresses*. A species that, like coracle-builders, must be almost extinct. We said 'au revoir' over a half-bottle of champagne from his mini-bar and I slipped out, into the rush hour, into normal life.

In St James's Park I pulled up the summer bedding. The plants came out easily. The packed earth beneath them was still pot-shaped; they had hardly rooted at all. It was a drizzly October; the next week we planted bulbs there and you would never have known the summer arrangement had existed. The House of Commons reconvened after its ludicrously long summer recess with two of its number replaced. The old, sexually-disgraced ones were Tories; the new ones were Lib-Dem. And Gavin announced that we had saved enough to install the central heating.

Which is how I came home one day, aching from double-digging, to discover him in a most un-Gavin-like state of excitement. He dragged me into the bedroom. 'What, *now*?' I said, 'but I'm filthy.'

I stopped and stared. Three of the floorboards had been removed, to install the radiator. Gavin held out a parcel wrapped in brown paper. 'Open it,' he said.

I opened it.

'Say something,' he said.

My throat closed up.

'Well?' He gazed at me. 'Well, Angie? Are we going to be honest?'

I paused. 'Honest?'

'Like, tell anyone. It must be someone's. Someone who lived here.'

I took a breath. 'Of course we won't tell. They don't belong to anyone we know.' I looked at my husband. 'We don't know anyone like that. Nobody like that would live here.'

So he sold the jewellery – they were real sapphires and real diamonds – and came home with £2,500. I got dressed up in my cheap Indian bangles from Camden Lock and we went out to dinner.

A curious thing happened. Over the next months Bertrand entered the bloodstream of our marriage. All summer he had been separate but now, for the first time, he came into our lives. He was there in the insouciance with which we bought a microwave, just like that; in our carefree lack of hesitation when we decided to go out to the movies; he was there in our flushed cheeks and heightened merriment when we drank a bottle of vintage Bordeaux. He was even there in our subsequent, wine-flushed lovemaking.

Our marriage did have roots, you see. We're still together, five years later. It did have roots, but my bearded, old-fashioned, middle-aged little Belgian – he helped it to flower.

Getting him Taped

I blame Mozart. Now, looking back on it. Well, it's easier to blame someone who's clever and dead, isn't it, than someone who's alive and foolish?

I blame Mozart, and the fact that nobody ever asks for his stuff, not where I work in the Holloway Road. It's all rap and hip-hop with us, and pimply youths shuffling around with dogs on strings, leaving cans of Special Brew on our Top Ten display case.

I blame the state I was in. Several peculiar things happened to me when my marriage broke up. Mozart made me cry. I lost seven pounds. I felt airily exhilarated, yet terrified. I felt stripped, like an onion, of several skins. I bought a calculator and learned how to tot up my Barclaycard. I became unnerved by main roads and sought refuge in supermarkets. I longed for a faceless man with strong arms to pull me to his chest, without saying a word. I longed for a man.

My ex wasn't a man; he was a neurotic. His exploration of his own psyche had desexed him and we had ended up like squabbling sisters. I was the one who ended up doing everything – changing lightbulbs, setting our incredibly complicated video recorder, carrying anything heavy because his back hurt. Oh yes, I blame my ex. Easier, that way.

It all started when this chap came in one day. He was older than me, mid-forties, and what I liked was the mess he was in. I mean, he was covered with plaster dust. His eyebrows and everything. He was wearing army trousers and an old jacket and was powdered all over. He was a big bloke, nice-looking, with huge hands which I watched when he paid. The tape looked so trivial in his palm. Outside he had an old van, crammed with planks from the timber yard opposite, and there he was buying a cassette of *Cosi Fan Tutte*. Somehow I had never connected builders with opera.

He came in the next week. It was pouring with rain. The shop was empty and I was eating coleslaw from a tub. He was scanning the Classical M – P and he gave me a wink, so I pointed to the tub with my plastic fork and said: 'The trouble with some things is, you go on eating and eating them and they never seem to get any less.'

He came over and looked at the tub. 'The trouble with coleslaw is that it's coleslaw.'

I laughed. It did seem a boring thing to eat. 'I don't know why I bought it,' I said. It was true – I had wandered round Marks & Spencer in my usual panic-stricken daze. Lately, decisions had seemed so tiring.

He went out of the shop, and in a moment he was back with a carrier bag he had got from his van. He fished about inside and produced some bread and Parma ham. 'Even got some tomatoes,' he said, taking out a pocket knife and slicing one.

That's how it all started, over crumbs and tomato pips and cassettes; and that's how it went on, over crumbs and cassettes and dust. I fell in love with him, helplessly, that first day when we sat on my desk with the rain sluicing down outside. His name was Hamish and he was doing up some properties in Islington.

I didn't call it love, then, because I didn't know if he would be coming back. But he did, and he took me to lunch at the kebab place down the road. I gazed at his hands – those hands! I felt he could sweep up my life, the debris of my life with all its failures; he could sweep it away and take care of me. His simple size helped. My ex,

Neil, had been smaller than me. Afterwards we sat in his van and *Cosi Fan Tutte* played while he stroked my thigh with his forefinger and said I was the nicest thing that had ever happened to him.

He was married, of course. Unhappily, and splitting-up, but he was still married. That's why we couldn't go back to his place. And he couldn't come home to mine because I had gone back to Ruislip to live with my parents – another admission of defeat, but only a temporary one. So his van became our everything – our dining room, our bedroom, our sealed, dusty little home. It smelt of turps. We sat on his overalls and ate tandoori chicken; I read him his horoscope in the paper. We talked for hours, he made words come into my head. The music was so beautiful and he unlocked me, as if I had never spoken before. I told him about the shops I had worked in and my awful parents. I told him about my marriage. We lay on his rags, bumping against tins of Creosote, and the windscreen steamed up with our breath.

We parked all over London, from EC1 to N6. He was always going to salvage yards for bits of railing or to obscure tile shops for obscure tiles. I'll tell you some of the places where we parked, they should add them to the London guidebooks. They could call them Erogenous Zones. There was the car park on Hampstead Heath, rendezvous for adulterers. Once I saw a couple in a Vaux-hall Cavalier; the woman was weeping. We parked facing those Georgian cottages that unimaginable people must be able to afford. I raised my head from Hamish's lap, my mouth wet with him, and gazed at their windows, fantasis-ing that someday it would be him and me living there. He would be painting the front door yellow and I would be happy. There was also the good old Inner Circle in Regents Park. Cabbies park there and eat sandwiches in their back seat; they visit each other like next-door neighbours. Those men were halo'ed with my joy, they were included in it. I can also recommend exclusive residential locations like the streets around Bishops Avenue because nobody walks there, they all drive. Wide, empty roads with just the odd Filipino cleaner going home, and they don't see anything. St John's Wood is good, too. Recently I walked down Carlton Hill and gazed at the Residents Parking Bay; there, for the first time, we climaxed together. Then there is the Embankment, with lorries flashing past and a view of the river. During the rush hour the traffic is so heavy you can be utterly private – in a van you can. Once we got a parking ticket, but neither of us noticed.

As I said, I talked about myself. He never told me much about what he did. 'You're rough trade,' I said, 'you're a builder. You should be wolf-whistling at women, not eating parma ham.'

'You're so buildist,' he murmured, licking my nipples. 'I'll have you up before the committee.'

'Never heard *my* plumber whistling *Fidelio*.'

'My dear, the world has changed. Haven't you noticed? Or were you too busy being married?'

'Tell me what you do.'

He said it was too boring, and once he started on about RSJs and planning applications I agreed. He never mentioned where he lived. His surname was Smith and I once looked up the H. Smiths in the phone book but there are five columns of them. He said it was too painful, to talk about all that. He and his wife were in the middle of a divorce; she had fallen for her Yoga instructor. Their place was on the market and in November he told me it was sold and he would be moving out in a couple of months.

'I want to live with you,' he said. He stroked my cheekbones and kissed my eyelids, one by one. 'I want to be all over you, up you and down you, here ... and here ...' And of course I wanted to live with him. I even told my parents I would be moving out.

We started looking for flats, but rather vaguely because

I think he really wanted a breathing space and who could blame him when his marriage had just fallen apart? For once I felt the superior, strong one. I told him he would recover. I had been there – through the dark valley and out into the sunlight uplands beyond. I came back, like an experienced guide, to urge him on and to lend him courage. 'You'll recover,' I said kindly. 'I promise.'

Sometimes I felt curious. Once I asked him the name of his street but he said: 'I don't want you to know. Can you understand? I don't want you to be connected to that – you're too precious. It's too messy.' I pictured his big hands sweeping all his own debris away. 'I want us to start again, new.'

But one day in early December he dropped in and bought £62.30 worth of CDs, for Christmas presents. We were busy and I couldn't serve him – my boss, Mr Karamarkos, did. When Hamish had gone the shop suddenly emptied and I had the most painful stab in my chest. I missed him. I felt dizzy with it and had to lean against the Popular Female Vocalists section. I longed to touch something that he had touched – have you ever felt like this? So when Mr Karamarkos went out I opened the till and took out Hamish's cheque. Tenderly I turned it over in my hand – his Midland Bank, his lovely looping signature. And on the back, guess what he had written, the cheque being for over £50? His address.

My heart, literally, jumped a beat. 26, Overton Street N1.

The first thing I did was rush to the newsagents next door and look it up in the *A-Z*. Overton Street. It was only a mile from the shop, over beyond Upper Street. You'll know how ill I was with love, how stupid, when I tell you how that shelf at the newsagents, the one with the *A-Z*s and the *Beano* annuals in it, possessed a magnetic glamour.

All the next day, Thursday, I resisted temptation. Hamish dropped in, briefly, to give me a box of liquorice allsorts – I was the only person he had ever met who liked them, and he said he found that endearing. But he was busy, there was some crisis at a site. 'My chippie's off sick, my bloody plumber's off sick and we're installing the central heating,' he said, and rushed out.

I felt so tenderly towards him that day. The discovery of his address made me feel more intimate with him, and the fact that he was unaware made me feel indulgent, as if he were a small boy who had made a secret camp in the shrubbery. That this place had been his marital home for the past seven years didn't disturb me as much as you might think. He was always insisting that he loved me more than he had ever loved his wife. He said she was mousy and overweight. He said he had married her because she had thought she was pregnant and her father had lent him the money to set up his business.

Savouring my suspense, like a boiled sweet I could suck for hours, I spent Thursday evening imagining what his place would look like. It wasn't easy. He was such a contradictory man – he had these refined tastes, like Mozart and the *Guardian,* and yet there he was, a builder, heaving joists about. No wonder I was besotted with him.

On Friday for some reason I felt nervous. Why hadn't he wanted me to know his address? Was he afraid I would go round and tell his wife? But that would make no sense. In a couple of weeks she would be out of the place, free to practice Yoga for the rest of her life, maybe it would help her weight problem. That was how bitchily dismissive I felt.

At lunchtime he came round and we sat in his van. He had just bought a cassette of *Don Giovanni* – I was starting to love opera now – and we ate Marks & Spencer cheese and celery sandwiches. I remember every mouthful, every word.

I mentioned nothing about my discovery. Secretly I had made a decision. The next day was Saturday. He didn't work Saturdays but I did. On my way to the shop I would go round and have a peep. It seemed more daring and interesting, somehow, that he might be at home. Maybe I could catch a glimpse of him.

I only had to take the bus three more stops than usual. On Saturday, at 8.45, I stepped off the bus and walked to Overton Street. My heart knocked against my ribs.

It was a surprisingly gentrified road – terraced houses with those whores' drawers curtains in the windows, Saabs parked outside. But it was his street – there stood his van, at the far end. I had expected to see a 'Sold' sign outside number 26 but there was none. I walked down to the end, on the other side of the road. I hid behind a Toyota Land Cruiser and looked across at number 26.

At first I didn't take it in. I really thought I had come to the wrong street. My sluggish brain couldn't catch up with the evidence before my eyes.

Number 26 was obviously being renovated. There was a skip outside, and a lot of planks stored in the basement. The house looked a wreck. There was somebody at the downstairs window, hard at work replacing the window frame. He was covered with dust and he didn't see me.

Just for a moment I thought: I've got it wrong. It's a job; he's working on Saturday, this isn't his place at all. My legs went weak; I squatted behind the Toyota.

Then I heard a voice. The front door opened and a woman came out. I peered through the Toyota's windows.

She was tall and striking, with red hair. She wore a boiler suit. She had obviously been working on the house too. At the van she stopped and called out: 'Anything else, darling?'

He leaned out of the open window and called back: 'Be an angel and get another tin of Nitromors.'

She groaned. They bickered with each other, nauseatingly, about the colour they were going to paint the hall and whether she should collect something from the Italian deli for their lunch – he suggested some ciabatta and mozzarella – and then she said: 'Remember, I need the van at six to visit Mum.'

They blew each other a kiss and she climbed into the van. I heard the swelling music as she inserted *Don Giovanni* and then she drove off.

I made it to the shop. I don't remember how. I worked, all morning, like a robot. Over and over in my head rolled the stupid words: he's not a builder at all. He's just doing up his own fucking house. For some reason, this was worse than the fact that he had lied about everything else.

In my lunch-break I went next door. Mr Khan, the newsagent, had a son with a ghetto blaster and I asked to borrow it. Then I returned to the shop, nicked one of our blank tapes and sat in the back room for half an hour.

At 5.45 I was back in Overton Street. It was dark and starting to rain. Number 26 had no curtains and I could see them, him and her, in the basement. They were unpacking shopping from Sainsbury's bags. She broke off a grape and popped it into his mouth.

I need the van at six to visit Mum. He never locked his van. I opened its door. Then I removed *Don Giovanni* from the cassette player – what an appropriate choice that had been – and slotted in my own personal tape. And then I hurried away.

At six o'clock she was in for a little suprise. Instead of that gorgeous aria *Inquali eccessi, o Numi* ('That ungrateful wretch betrayed me') – instead of Donna Elvira, she was going to hear my own melodious tones.

My name is Joyce. I first met your husband when he came into my shop to buy a tape. 'How could you eat coleslaw?' he said, and fetched us some parma ham . . .

And I'm going back to the Rolling Stones.

Lucky Dip

The point of raffles is that you never win. You don't expect to, do you? It's like the Pools; it happens to somebody else.

In fact, by the end of the evening I had forgotten I had even bought a ticket. This happened last January, at a Firestone Tyres Dinner. I had gone with a mate of mine, also in the motor trade. His girlfriend had tonsillitis, so he had asked me to go instead and I thought: why not? During cocktails I had bought a ticket, they practically forced you. It was on behalf of something worthy – Distressed Vauxhall-Owners, the Old Alvis Sanctuary, I didn't really hear. I had forgotten all about the ticket, in the pocket of my hired DJ. When they read out the number it sounded unfamiliar, like a bus route you don't take, and then – thump – I suddenly realized it was mine. First Prize.

I had to walk up to a platform and meet an actress. You might have recognized her; somebody said she played a vet's assistant on afternoon TV. People started clapping and she gave me an envelope. Just for a moment the room echoed and the faces shrank. Fame at last. It was a holiday for two in Portugal.

Chance. A hand gropes in a hat, the fingers touch a scrap of paper. I run a garage, you see – Chiswick Lane Autos. Victims of chance are our stock-in-trade. A chance collision, metal against metal, the crunch of two innocent little errands and bang. Usually I'm too busy to realize the randomness of it all, but sometimes I straighten up, oily and awe-struck.

So an actress had groped in a hat and given me a week in the Algarve. Trouble was, the two.

Now, a romantic holiday in Portugal is just the ticket if you've got somebody to be romantic with. Since my divorce I'd had one or two girlfriends but the whole thing had been vaguely unsatisfactory, probably due to me. I had been humiliated and, like a car-crash, if you've had one you drive more carefully for a while. Just slipping into the front seat, you're aware of the possibilities. This makes for a tentative expedition.

I couldn't call them up again. 'Remember me, Desmond? How about a rekindling week at the Manicharo Apartments, courtesy of Sunspan Holidays?' I didn't even know their phone numbers unless I rang their parents, and I only knew one lot of those. The whole idea was pathetic. So was taking my sister, who was a chiropodist in Finchley and longing for a jaunt. Blokes were out of the question, needless to say. I would never live it down.

Two dates were offered for the holiday – March and November. For the first few months I refused to panic. There was plenty of time. It seemed so far away that I was actually looking forward to it. Didn't I deserve a break? Something, someone, somehow, would turn up.

March came and went, blustery and cold. April, May and then June, blustery and somehow colder. By August I was starting to get anxious.

I couldn't confide in Norm. He's the bloke I work with, and he's been married for thirty-three years. Besides, his wife's got a hip and he spends his lunch-breaks doing the shopping. Norm is not the responsive type; he collects tropical fish. He thinks I'm an intellectual because I read Dick Francis.

Then there was Robbie. He's in the next premises and he does our panel-beating. Single-handed, he's kept the property prices down in this locality; in fact, with a brisk west wind you can hear him on Ealing Broadway. Robbie's office is wallpapered with wet t-shirt calendars from sparking plug firms. He wasn't the ideal person for a delicate conversation of this nature.

I couldn't possibly go on holiday by myself; not when it was a prize. They would be expecting a loving couple; the manager would greet us with a wink and a bowl of fruit. I had been away alone, of course, but only to lowly-sexed locations like the Lake District. Portugal was sun and sand and sangria. I've been to Spain, you see. Twice. I'm not a total wimp.

As the months dragged on I even considered, for a mad moment, giving it a miss altogether. There was a beauty salon I had passed in the Uxbridge Road, when I went to tow away a Toyota. It offered sun beds. I could take a week off and return to Chiswick Lane Autos mahogany and smug. I could play it mysterious and keep Robbie on tenterhooks.

However, there was my own self-esteem to think of. I did have some left. By this time I had forgotten that the whole thing was supposed to be pleasant. By now it was just something to be got through, willy-nilly. To tell the truth, by now anyone would do.

Female customers were the only other possibility. The trouble with them was my invisibility. To most of them I was just some geezer in greasy overalls who presented them with a bill for about twice as much as they'd expected – that's what happens with garage bills, what with the VAT and whatnot.

There were some I liked, of course. There was one girl with a temperamental Metro – a contradiction in terms, with a Metro, but you hadn't seen her clutch-abuse. She actually knew my name, Desmond, and we had had some interesting conversations about Alfred Hitchcock because she was a film buff. Then there was a flirtatious type with a 2CV, the lentil-eater's car. Unlike our other 2CV customers, however, this one wore a mini-skirt and had a terrific pair of legs. But how could I manage the jump from 'It's passed its MOT,' to 'What about a holiday for two in Portugal?'

Anyway, they were mostly married. It was Thomas the Tank Engine cassettes on the floor and Mrs on their cheques. The only other possibility was a Ms Hodges, who drove an Escort XR3. But she had a carphone, which I somehow found intimidating. I know most men wouldn't, but there you go.

Still, attraction was no longer my first priority. Not even a consideration, really. Anybody able-bodied, female gender, under sixty, would do. By the end of August, Robbie was getting leery. 'Go on. Give us a butchers, you sly bugger.'

And then, on August 21st, Tina came in with her Capri. It was a flash job – 2.8, alloy wheels, spoilers, two-tone champagne/silver, the works. She had pranged its bonnet.

'They shouldn't have made it a one-way street,' she said irritably.

I thought it was a surprising car for her to drive, but you get some funny matches, with motors. Like marriage, really.

She dropped in the next day, on the off-chance it was ready (it wasn't). 'I only work up the road,' she said, 'at Hair Today. It's no trouble.'

I was under the hood of a Cavalier, wrestling with a brake pad. I came out and wiped my hands. 'Fancy a lager?' I asked. Suddenly summer had started, and I was sweltering.

She nodded. It was lunchtime, and Norm had gone off to buy some pond weed. We sat down on a couple of oil drums. After we had opened the Heinekens, a silence fell. It always does just then, doesn't it.

'Been on your holidays yet?' she asked, and giggled.

'Where I work, it's what you get asked half the year. The other half it's – '

'What are you doing for Christmas?'

She laughed. Like most hairdressers her own hair was a real mess – bleached bits growing out. She was very pretty, and sort of frayed around the edges in a vaguely promising way. Her slingbacks were trodden down at the back and she had a little crucifix around her neck; I remembered from my younger days that this was a good sign. Girls wearing them were invariably goers.

Luckily I didn't have to answer about the holidays because Robbie came over to tell her how much it would cost to knock out the dents in her Capri, and she rolled her eyes.

When she had gone he rolled his. 'Wouldn't mind fiddling under *her* bonnet,' he said.

In October she came back again. This time she had dented the back bumper of the car, and crunched the boot. 'I was only putting on me brakes,' she said. 'The silly cow wasn't looking.'

It was raining, so we sat in the office and had a cup of coffee. Today she had re-bleached her hair and it was tied up in a plastic comb. She looked young and ripe.

'So what are you doing for Christmas?' I asked.

She laughed. 'Haven't even had me hols yet. I was going to the Canaries with my friend Beverley, but she went off with a married man and I couldn't go alone, could I?'

'I know the feeling,' I said. Then I took a breath. There was a silence, broken by a tattoo of hammer-blows from next door.

'Ever fancied Portugal?'

So off we went, 5 a.m. on a November morning, Gatwick to Faro. Tina sat beside me, wearing a yellow t-shirt and pink slacks. She had even brought along a straw hat; she looked ready for anything. 'Hair today, gone tomorrow,' she laughed. 'Is me lipstick wonky? It was pitch bloody dark when we left.'

As the plane lifted I felt dizzy with the chanciness of it all. If the girlfriend hadn't got tonsillitis; if the actress had picked another raffle ticket; if that other car had arrived one second later and Tina hadn't bumped into it . . . my palms were clammy. What on earth were we going to do?

'What are you thinking?' she asked.

I jumped. 'I was just wondering where bank notes go when they get old. Like, do they just get dirtier and dirtier and fall to bits, and the last person's the unlucky one?'

She burst out laughing. 'I can see this is going to be a hoot.'

The Manicharo Apartments was a high-rise building surrounded by bulldozers. Skyscrapers were being built all around us; the air was filled with hammering and drilling. It was like a hundred Robbies, out there. We went to our room.

'For the happy couple!' shouted the manager, giving us our starter pack. This had bread rolls in it, and little packets of Nescafé. I edged towards the bedroom and peered in. Twin beds.

It was off-season and the place was deserted except for six old dears who were sitting around the pool. They eyed us with interest when we joined them.

'I'm from Melton Mowbray,' said one of them, who had spread her tapestry over three sunloungers. 'But we always come here for the winter, don't we Dot?'

Out in the street the drilling started. Dot shouted: 'It's nice to see some fresh young faces, isn't it?' She turned to us. 'There's bingo tonight, it's all go, then it's whist tomorrow, and your last night it's Sangria'n'Disco.'

Tina had stripped down to her bikini. She was anointing

herself with Ambre Solaire. She had a lovely body, plump-
ish and compact.

'Wonder what Vic's going to say,' she murmured, lying
back.

'Vic?'

'About the bills for the car. It's his.'

'Who's Vic?' I asked.

'My boyfriend.' She closed her eyes.

Three days passed. We sat beside the pool and inspected
the range of teabags in the local supermarket. We played
ping-pong in the deserted concrete games room and had
free drinks with time-share touts. It was about three miles
to the sea, through building sites, but at least it was an
expedition. One of the places on the beach was open, and
it served chips.

The whole business wasn't quite as I had expected, but
Tina didn't seem to mind. She had turned a shy pink, and
freckles appeared on her nose. At night, after the evening's
entertainment downstairs, we modestly changed into our
pyjamas, she in the bathroom and me in the bedroom, and
climbed into our twin beds. Then we read our books –
luckily I had brought enough for two. Outside in the corri-
dor we heard the clunk-clunk of Ruby's walking frame as
she made her way back from the bar.

On the Wednesday Tina put down her John Le Carré;
she had forgotten which spy was which. 'Tell me about
your wife,' she said.

'Ex,' I corrected. 'She worked in the perfumery department at Selfridges, squirting aftershave at strange men. I
knew it was a mistake.'

'What happened?'

'One day she scored a direct hit. It was a sheik. She ran
away with him back to wherever it was, Saudi Arabia,
somewhere horrible. I've never known.'

There was a pause. Outside, the drilling had stopped. Sometimes it seemed to go on all night.

'Tell me about Vic,' I said.

'Oh, he's in prison.'

I paused. 'What for?'

'GBH.'

'What's that?'

'Grievous bodily harm.'

'I knew it was,' I said. 'Just making sure.'

'Nighty-night.' She switched off her light. 'Don't let the bedbugs bite.'

By the next day she was turning a faint but delicious shade of honey. The sun was weak and the days short but she was determined to get a tan. We lay beside the pool. I had graduated to rubbing her with suntan oil.

'Mmm . . .' she murmured into her towel. 'A bit lower . . .'

'Have you two lovebirds tried the supermarket opposite Spud'U'Like?' shouted Ruby, above the noise. 'Their *Daily Telegraph*'s only a day late.'

I went on rubbing oil onto Tina's firm, stocky thighs. My mouth was dry with desire. But if it happened, and it wasn't a success, how were we going to get through the next three days? And did she want it, anyway? Above all, what about Vic? I pictured him attacking me – a Robbie hammering at my helpless bodywork.

'When's he coming out?' I asked. 'From, you know?'

'Vic? The week after we get back.'

Our last night was Sangria'n'Disco. The Sunspan rep, a jovial heterosexual called Malcolm, filled and refilled our glasses. Afterwards a combo played and we danced the hokey-cokey with Dot and Co. I gripped frail, boney arms. Ruby's diamanté top slipped off her shoulder. I hitched it up for her and twirled her round; how light and papery she was, as brittle as a bird! A blink, and this week was finished . . . this, and the next, and the next. Disappeared and gone for ever. I clutched Ruby in my arms; I smelt her talcum powder. Dancing with her, I heard the faint, roaring sound of time passing – a far-off roar, like the sea down the road. We drank some more and sang that song: *With a little bit of this . . .* We wiggled our fingers . . . *And a little bit of that . . .*

'And a little bit of the other,' leered Malcolm, 'for the lucky ones.'

Finally there was a slow number. The ladies got out their knitting. To the accompaniment of clicking needles I drew Tina close and breathed in the chlorine scent of her hair.

'I want to leave him,' she murmured. 'But you can't, when they're doing Time.'

'That's what we're all doing,' I said, glancing at the other residents.

'In that place, they've only got their hopes and dreams to keep them going.'

'So have we.'

'Anyway, he's got my name tattooed somewhere special, and it's ever so painful to get it removed. Specially there.' We shuffled a few steps. 'How could he get another girl-friend? The name would be wrong.'

That night, inflamed by alcohol, I kissed her. Finally we stumbled into my twin bed.

Afterwards she stroked my cheek. 'Know something?' she whispered. 'Your wife was daft.'

That was a month ago. It's a funny thing, about love. Things slot into place around you, your happiness makes that happen. They slot into place like smooth, polished pieces of joinery. Maybe your charmed life disarms people. Maybe your warm breath melts away the jagged edges, like sunlight melting ice. I don't know. All I know is that what happened with Vic didn't surprise me as much as I had expected. The circumstances, maybe, but not the outcome.

See, he came out of prison a changed man. Apparently they had had a visiting creative writer, at the Scrubs, and Vic went to see him because it meant skiving laundry rota. He had ended up writing a poem, something about the bird of freedom beating its wings, and it had won the Arthur Koestler prize – £200! – for something arty done whilst behind bars.

When he came out he was a bit of a celebrity, and much in demand at writers' circles where he charmed genteel ladies with his virile good looks. From what I've heard, those gatherings are like the Manicharo Apartments – most of their regulars are old dears.

One of them, however, was reasonably young. She was aiming for Mills and Boon and he must have seemed like something straight out of those sort of books – a dream come true. Tina and I met him in Acton, for a drink. His new girlfriend was sitting beside him. She wore glasses and an Indian thing with a fringe round the bottom.

I thought of his tattoo. 'Don't tell me,' I said to the new girlfriend. 'Let me guess your name.'

She put down her shandy and said coyly: 'Go on then.'

'It begins with a T.'

She shook her head. 'C.'

Vic took out his cigarettes. 'It's Christina,' he said, stroking her knee.

Beside me, Tina exploded with giggles. 'You mean, that's the long version.'

The girl nodded. 'Oh yes. It's Tina for short.'

Empire Building

It didn't look much when he took it over, the Empire Stores, but a man with business instinct could see the potential. The previous owners had been fined by the Health Authority and finally gone bust. Hamid, however, had standards. His wife told people this too, with a small shake of her head as if she were being philosophical about it.

The neighbourhood was a transient, shabby one, with terraces of bedsits and Irish lodging houses. The parade of shops, Hamid calculated, was far enough from the Holloway Road for people to rely upon it for their local needs, which he had all intention of supplying. The shops were as follows: a wholesale dressmaking business with a curtained window behind which the sewing machines hummed – those Greek ladies knew the meaning of hard work; a dentist's surgery with frosted glass; a greengrocer's that had ageing fruit and early closing on Thursday – now how can anyone prosper with early closing; then the Empire Stores, and next door to it a newsagent's run by an indolent Hindu and his wife. Hamid put a notice UNDER NEW MANAGEMENT in the window of the Empire Stores and re-stocked the merchandise – liquor behind the cash desk, where he sat in control, and groceries along the aisles. His aims were not modest, but his beginnings were.

His own wife and children were installed in a flat in Wood Green, three miles away, where the air was fresher and the neighbourhood more salubrious. The streets around the Empire Stores were not respectable; you need only have taken a look at the cards fixed to the newsagent's window – even a family man like Hamid knew the meaning of those kind of French Lessons. Business is business, however, and it is a wise shop keeper who is prepared to adapt. Or, as his father was fond of saying: to those who are flexible comes strength.

The local blacks were big West Indians who drove up in loudly tuned cars and who suddenly filled the shop. They bought party packs of beer in the evenings and left a musky male scent behind them. One of the first things Hamid did was to extend his opening hours until 9 p.m. Then there were the single young ladies who bought Whiskas and yoghurt and disappeared into the sodium-lit streets. How solitary was the life of these young English women with no family to care for them; no wonder they fell into evil ways. Hamid installed a second cold shelf and stocked it with pizzas, two ranges of yoghurts and individual fruit-juice cartons for these bedsit dwellers and their twilit lives. Such items moved fast.

Sitting at the till, its numbers bleeping, Hamid thought of the dinner being prepared for him at home – the hiss of the spices as they hit the pan, the buttery taste of the paratha he would soon be eating. He thought of his son Arif, his neat, shiny head bent over his homework, the TV turned right down. He thought of his own tartan slippers beside the radiator. Passing them a carrier-bag, he gazed with perplexity at these lost, pasty-faced English girls.

His main income, however, came from the drunks. It was for them that within the first three months he had doubled the bottle shelf-space and increased his range of cans. Business was brisk in Triple Strength Export Lager. These men, their complexions inflamed by alcohol, shambled in at all hours, muttering at the floor, murmuring at the tins of peas. They raised their ruined faces. Hamid avoided their eyes; he took their soiled bank notes or the coins they counted out, shakily, and fixed his gaze above their heads. Flesh upon flesh, sometimes their fingers touched his, but he was too well-mannered to flinch. Sometimes they tried to engage him in conversation.

It was bemusing. Not only did they poison themselves with drink, rotting their souls and their bodies, but they had no shame. They leaned against the dentist's frosted glass, lifting the bottle to their lips in full public view. They stood huddled together in the exit of the snooker hall, further up the road, where warm air breathed from the grilles. Sometimes he could hear the smash of glass. Lone men stood in the middle of the road, shouting oaths into the air.

Business is business. Sometimes he raised his eyebrows at Khalid, his nephew, who helped him in the shop, but he never offended his wife by describing to her this flotsam and jetsam. One night she said: 'You never talk to me.'

It was the next week that a man stumbled in and steadied himself against the counter. He asked for a bottle of cider and then he said: 'You'll put it on the slate?'

'I beg your pardon?' Hamid raised his eyes from his newspaper.

'I'll pay tomorrow.'

'I'm sorry,' Hamid said. 'It is not shop policy.'

The man started shouting. 'You fucking wog!' he yelled, his voice rising.

Hamid lowered his gaze back to the dancing Urdu script. He turned the page.

'Get back to the fucking jungle, fucking wog land!' the voice slurred – 'where you belong!'

Khalid appeared from the stock-room and stood there. Hamid kept his eye on the page. He read that there was a riot in Lahore, where an opposition leader had been arrested, and that ghee was up Rs 2 per seer.

'Fucking monkeys!'

Khalid put down the crate of Schweppes and escorted

the man to the door. The next day Hamid wrote a notice and Sellotaped it to the counter.

He sat there, as grave as always, in his herringbone tweed jacket. He held himself straight as the men shambled in, those long-lost rulers of a long-lost Empire, eyeing the bottles behind him. He had written the notice in large red letters, using Arif's school Pentel: PLEASE DO NOT ASK FOR CREDIT AS A REFUSAL OFTEN OFFENDS.

That was in the late seventies. War was being waged in the Middle East; a man had walked on the moon; Prince Charles had still not found a wife. Meanwhile Hamid filled out his VAT receipts, and in view of increased turnover negotiated further discount terms with McEwans, manufacturers of lager.

In 1980 the old couple who ran the greengrocer's retired and Hamid bought the shop, freehold, and extended his own premises, knocking through the dividing wall and removing the sign H. LAWSON FRUITERER AND GREEN-GROCER.

Apart from 'good morning', the first and last conversation he ever held with the old man was on completion day, when they finalized the transaction in the lawyer's office down the road.

'Times change,' said the old man, Mr Lawson. The clock whirred, clicked and chimed. He sighed. 'Been here thirty years.'

They signed the document and shook hands.

'Harold,' said Hamid, reading the signature. 'So that's your name.'

'You know, I was in your part of the world.'

'My part?' asked Hamid.

'India.'

'Ah.'

'In the army. Stationed near Mysore. Know it?'

Hamid shook his head. 'My family comes from Pakistan.'

They stood up. 'Funny old world, isn't it,' said the old man.

Hamid agreed, politely. The lawyer opened the door for them.

'How about a quickie,' said the old man.

'I beg your pardon?'

'Little celebration.'

Hamid paused. 'I don't drink.'

They reached the head of the stairs. 'No,' said the old man. 'No, I suppose you don't. Against your religion, eh?'

Hamid nodded. 'You first, please,' he said, indicating the stairs.

'No, you.'

Hamid went first. They emerged into the sunlight. It was a beautiful day in April. Petals lay strewn in the gutter.

'If I'd been blessed with a son, maybe this wouldn't be happening,' said the old man. 'But that's life.'

Hamid nodded.

'You've got a son?'

'Yes,' said Hamid. 'A fine chap.'

'Expect he'll be coming in with you, in due course.'

Hamid murmured something politely; he didn't want to offend the old man. Arif, running a shop? He had greater things in mind for his son.

Hamid had a new, larger sign fitted to cover the new, double shop-front and this time had it constructed in neon-illuminated script: THE EMPIRE STORES.

He extended both his liquor and grocery range to cover the extra volume of retail space, adding a chicken rotisserie for take-outs, a microwave for samosas and a large range of fruit and vegetables – all of a greatly improved quality to those of H. Lawson. The old man had left the place like a junk heap; it took seven skips to clear the rubbish out of the upper floor and the backyard. One morning Hamid was out in the street, inspecting a heaped skip, when one of his customers stopped. She was an old woman; she pointed at the skip with her umbrella.

'See that?' she said. 'The wheels? Used to have a pony and cart, Harry did. For the deliveries.'

'Did he really?' Hamid glanced up the street. He was waiting for the builders who were late again. Unreliable.

'Knew us all by name.' She sighed and wiped her nose. 'No . . .' She shook her head. 'Service is not what it was.'

'No,' agreed Hamid, looking at his watch and thinking of his builders. 'It certainly isn't.'

Hamid, who always bought British, traded in his old Cortina and bought a brand-new Rover, with beige upholstery and stereo-player. He transferred Arif to a private school, its sign painted in Gothic script, where they sang hymns and wore blazers. On Parents' Day the panelled halls smelt of polish; Hamid gazed at the cabinets of silver cups. His wife wore her best silk sari; her bangles tinkled as she smoothed Arif's hair.

The conversion of the upper floors, above the old fruit shop, was completed at last and Hamid stood on the other side of the street with Khalid and his two new assistants. He looked at the sunlight glinting in the windows; he looked at the dazzling white paint and the sign glowing below it: THE EMPIRE STORES. His heart swelled. The others chattered, but he could not speak.

That night Arif stood, his eyes closed and his face pinched with concentration, and recited:

> *'Earth has not anything to show more fair:*
> *Dull would he be of soul who could pass by*
> *A sight so touching in its majesty:*

This City now doth, like a garment, wear
The beauty of the morning; silent, bare,
Ships, towers, domes, theatres, and temples lie
Open unto the fields, and to the sky;'

His eyes opened. 'Know who it's by?'

Hamid shook his head. 'You tell me, son.'

'William Wordsworth. We're learning it at school.'

For the second time that day, Hamid's heart swelled. He put his arms around his son, the boy for whom everything was possible. He pressed his face against his son's cheek.

1981. Ronald Reagan became President of the USA. In May the Pope was shot and wounded. In Brixton there were riots; Toxteth too. In July Prince Charles married his Lady Di.

Khalid, too, was married by now and installed in the first-floor flat above the shop. National holidays were always good, business-wise; by now the Empire Stores was open seven days a week and during that summer's day, as people queued at the till, Hamid kept half an eye on his portable TV set. A pale blur, as Lady Di passed in her dress; a peal of bells. As Hamid reached for the bottles of whiskey, the commentator's voice quickened with pride and awe. Hamid's heart beat faster. 'Isn't she a picture,' said his customers, pausing at the screen. Hamid agreed that, yes, she was the most radiant of brides. Flags waved, flicking to and fro and the crowd roared. Our Princess, his and theirs . . . Hamid smiled and gave a small boy a Toblerone.

That night his wife said: 'You should have seen it in colour.'

Hamid pulled off his shoes. 'You've put it on the video-tape?'

She nodded and turned away, picking up the scattered

jigsaw in front of the TV, where his daughters had been sitting.

'We can watch it later,' he said.

'When?' Her voice was sharp. He looked up in surprise. 'It's not the same,' she said, closing the box.

That night a bottle was thrown up through the window of Khalid's flat. It shattered the glass; Khalid's bride cowered in the corner.

The next day, while the Royal couple – oh how happy they looked – departed on their honeymoon, Hamid inspected the damage. He gazed down into the street, through the wicked edges of glass. They were intruders, those people entering the Empire Stores. Yesterday's glory had vanished. Hamid sat down heavily, on the settee.

'How could they do this to us?' he asked. 'What have we done to deserve it?'

Khalid, who was an easy-going young man, said: 'Forget it. They were just celebrating.' He lowered his voice, so his bride couldn't hear. 'They were one over the eight.'

'What?'

'Drunk.'

Drunk on the drink he had sold to them. Yesterday he had had record takings.

He closed up the shop that night and walked to his car. On the pavement lay a man, asleep, his face bleeding. Cans lay around him. Hamid remembered how once, years ago, he had called an ambulance when he had found a person in this state.

Now he just made a detour on the other side of the pavement.

That autumn he installed closed-circuit surveillance in the shop. He now had three assistants and an expanded range of take-away food. Children from neglectful homes came in with shopping bags; they had keys around their necks, and runny noses. They bought bars of Kit Kat and crisps and hot pasties. These mothers did not look after their youngsters; they sent them into the streets to consume junk food.

The dressmaker's was taken over by a massage and sauna establishment, which installed black glass and a Georgian door. All about lay the ruined and the dispossessed. This was their country but these people had no homes. New, loitering men replaced the old. Strange faces appeared for a week, a month, and then after a while he would realize they had vanished. To where? His neon sign shone out over the drab street. Inside the shop lay the solace of food, and order.

That year his turnover doubled. He fitted out an office in the store-room and managed his growing empire from there, drinking tea from his Charles and Di commemoration mug. He had now converted four flats above the shop, and the lease of the newsagent's shop next door was coming up shortly; he had his eye on that.

In an attempt to brighten the neighbourhood, the council had planted young trees along the pavement. Their leaves were turning red and falling to the ground. Opposite, the sunset flamed above the chimney-pots. As he said his evening prayers on the mat behind his desk, he felt both humbled and grateful.

That evening he looked into his girls' bedroom. They were two sleeping heads. Arif was in the lounge, bent over his computer game. Hamid ruffled his hair; Arif smoothed it down again.

'And have you a hello for your father?'

Arif pressed a button. '570,' he said. '680.'

Later, when Arif was asleep and Hamid had eaten, he said to his wife: 'They teach them no manners at that expensive school?'

She turned, 'You think you can buy manners with money?'

He looked sharply at her. She was putting the crockery away in the cabinet.

'What are you trying to say?' he asked.

'Manners are taught by example. At home.'

'And don't I set a good example?'

'When you're here.' She sighed, and shut the cabinet. 'I think he is suffering from neglect.'

'You say that about my son?'

Neglect? Hamid thought of the boys with faces like old men's, and keys around their necks. Pale boys buying junk food.

'It's his age,' said Hamid loudly, surprising himself. 'He's fourteen now. A difficult age.'

'If you say so.'

She sighed again and reached up for something on the top of the cabinet. It was a box of Milk Tray. How plump she was becoming; her kurta was strained tight over her belly.

'Come to the shop,' he said, 'and there I'll show you the meaning of neglect.'

She sat down, shaking her head in that philosophical way. More and more she irked him by doing this. She examined a chocolate and popped it into her mouth. He looked at her and the word rose up: junk food.

He ignored this. Instead he asked: 'Doesn't Arif understand? I'm working for him. For all the family.' He ran his fingers through his hair. 'For the future.' His voice rose higher. She glanced warningly towards the bedrooms. 'I'm working so that he need never work in a shop! You understand me, woman? Can't you understand?'

She said nothing, though she tilted her head. He thought she was assenting, but then he saw she was just choosing another chocolate.

Hindus are lazy. History has proved that point. Their religion is a dissipated one; their life-style one of self-indulgence, of the inaction that comes from fatalism. Take Mr Gupta's attitude, for example, to the expiry of his lease. He smiled and raised his hands: the new price was too high; he had this trouble with his stomach; he had been robbed three times in the past year. What will be, will be . . .

Hamid would have suggested that Mr Gupta invest in vandal-proof shuttering, as he himself had done. But he could always have that fitted when he took over the lease, which he did just as the trees outside frothed into blossom, in celebration.

Islam is a progressive faith. He progressed, removing Mr Gupta's sign and installing THE EMPIRE NEWSAGENTS over the door. He now had one double shop and one single; his properties dominated the parade of shops. Indeed, that week several of his customers joked that he'd soon be taking over the street. Hamid smiled modestly.

The state of that shop! The squalor and the unexploited sales area! The possibilities! It was a dusty little con-tob newsagent's when Hamid took it over, but after a complete refitment he had doubled the shelf space and the stock, and introduced fast-profit items including a rental Slush-Puppy dispenser in six flavours – a favourite with the local latch-key children.

Dirty magazines, he was not surprised to discover, had a brisk sale in this neighbourhood and he increased the stock from seven titles to fourteen. *Knave* and *Mayfair*, bulging flesh . . . he kept his eyes from this nude shamelessness. He placed such journals on the top shelf. Boys little older than Arif came in to giggle and point; they stood in a row on his display bases. These boys, he thought, they are somebody's son; does nobody cherish and protect them?

It was during the first month of business that Hamid opened the local newspapers and read: 'We are sad to announce the death of Mr Harold Lawson, universally known as Harry to his customers and many friends. For thirty years he was a well-loved sight on the local scene, with the fondly remembered Betty, his pony . . .'

Hamid read on. It concluded: 'A modest man, he seldom mentioned his distinguished army record, serving with the King's Rifles in India and being awarded a DSO for his bravery during the Independence Riots. He leaves a widow, Ivy, and will be sorely missed. It can truly be said that "they broke the mould when they made Harry".'

Outside the petals had blown into the gutter, just as they had lain the day Hamid had accompanied the old man into the street two years earlier. It was the slack mid-morning period and Hamid stood in the sunshine, watching the clouds move beyond the TV aerials. For a moment he thought of the earth rolling, and history turning. He himself was fond of poetry, despite his lack of education. What was it Arif used to recite? 'Deign on the passing world to turn thine eyes,/And pause awhile from letters to be wise.'

That evening he asked Arif who was the English poet who had written those words. William Shakespeare?

'Dunno.'

Hamid placed his hand on his son's shoulder. 'No, that's "All the world's a stage",' he said. Arif's bones were surprisingly frail. He sat with his eyes on the TV screen where first a house, then a car, burst into flames.

Hamid kept his son's exercise books on a special shelf. He searched through and found the quotation, written in the round, careful writing Arif still had a year or so ago.

'Ah. Samuel Johnson.'

Hamid raised his voice; on the TV a siren wailed.

'Remember?'

He looked at the title: *The Vanity of Human Wishes*.

Arif said: 'You're blocking my view.'

1983. Renewed fighting in the Lebanon, and the film

Gandhi won eight Oscars. There were fires and floods in Australia and peace people made a human chain around Greenham Common. The future King of England was toddling now, so was Khalid's first-born son in the flat above the Empire Stores. Property was moving again, as the worst of the recession was said to be over, and Hamid converted the upper floors above the newsagent's shop and sold the flats on long leases.

With the profits, and another bank loan, that summer he bought a large detached house for his family, a real family home in that sought-after suburb, Potters Bar.

'I have worked twenty years for this moment,' he said, standing in the lounge. There were fitted carpets throughout. There was even a bar in panelled walnut, built by the previous owners who had amassed large debts both by drinking and gambling, hence the sale of this house. He pictured his children sitting around the bar, drinking blameless Pepsi.

'This is the proudest moment of my life,' he repeated, his words loud in the empty room. Through its french windows there was a view of the garden, a series of low terraces separated by balustrades. Two small figures in orange anoraks stood on the lawn: his daughters.

Arif, however, was nowhere to be seen. Hamid would have liked him to share this moment but his son had been keeping himself to himself recently, growing more sulky. He had even objected to the move.

'Where will we get the furniture?' said his wife, standing in the middle of the room.

'We'll buy it. Look.' He took out his wallet. It was so fat, it couldn't close.

He found Arif sitting in the car, the radio loud. Hamid turned it down.

'Well, old chap,' he said. 'What do you think?'

'Great,' Arif muttered.

169

'Earth has not anything to show more fair: . . .'

Hamid stood in the garden. The long, blond grass blew in the wind. It was dusk and he looked up at his home, the fortress where he kept his family safe. A light shone from Arif's attic bedroom – he had insisted on this tiny room, no more than a cupboard up in the roof. Down below were the bedrooms; then, below them, the curtained french windows, glowing bluish from the TV. How solid his house, solid and secure.

Today he wore his tweed suit from Austin Reed. He stood like a squire amidst the swaying weeds. Summer was ending now, and grass choked the flowerbeds. Neither he nor his wife were proficient in gardening, but that did not stop the pride.

It grew darker. To one side of him rose the block of his house. To the other side, beyond the trees, the sky glowed orange. This side lay London. He thought of his shops casting their own glow over the pavement; he thought of the blood-red neon of THE EMPIRE STORES shining in the night. How ashy those faces seemed, looking up at the window to gaze at the comforts within! Ruined, pasty faces; the losers, the lost, the dispossessed. The walking wounded who once ruled the Empire, pressing their noses against his Empire Stores . . .

He thought of their squalid comforts: those rows of bottles and those magazines showing bald portions of women's bodies. Here at home, on the other hand, he had a mahogany bookcase filled with English classics, all of them bound in leather: Dickens, Shakespeare and the poet he had taken to his own heart: William Wordsworth.

The trees, bulkier now in the night, loomed against the suffused sky. 'Dull would he be of soul who could pass by / A sight so touching in its majesty. . .'

A chill wind rattled the weeds and blew against his legs. He heard the faint thump of music, if you could call it music, from Arif's window. The long, dry grass blew to and fro in the darkness. He realized that he was shivering.

His wife said she was lonely. She sat in the lounge, its new chairs arranged for conversations, and all day she had the TV on. She talked about Lahore; she said she was home-sick. She talked about her sisters, and how they had sat all morning laughing and brushing each other's hair. More and more she talked like this.

'Nobody talks to me here,' she said. 'They get into their cars and drive to their tea parties.'

'You must take driving lessons.'

'The car is so big. It frightens me.'

'Then you must have a tea party here.'

She thought about this for some time. Then she said: 'Who shall I invite?'

'The neighbours, of course. And then there are the parents of Arif's schoolfriends.'

'But we don't know the parents of Arif's schoolfriends.'

'What about that boy, what's his name, Thompson? His father is an executive with Proctor & Gamble.'

'But what shall I cook for them?'

'And that very pleasant couple next door? We've said good morning often enough, and discussed the state of the hedge.'

So it was arranged. A small party for Sunday tea, so that he himself could be present.

For the next week she was restless; she moved about the house, frowning at the furniture and standing back from it, her head on one side. During one evening she moved the settee three times. She took Arif down to Marks & Spencers to buy him a new pair of trousers.

'Christ,' said Arif. 'It's only a bloody tea party.'

'Don't you dare insult your mother!' Hamid's voice was shrill. He, too, moved the settee one more time.

The question of food was vexing. His wife thought sandwiches and cake most suitable. He himself thought she should produce those titbits in which she excelled: pakoras, bringal fritters and the daintiest of samosas. Nobody cooked samosas like his Sharine.

In the end they compromised. They would have both.

'East meets West,' he joked; his nerves made him high-spirited. He joggled the plaits of Aisha, his youngest daughter; one plait and then the other, and she squealed with pleasure. 'East, West, home's best,' he chanted to her, before she scuttled into the kitchen.

He wanted to tell his family how much he loved them, and how proud he would be to show them off at the tea party. He wanted to tell them how he had stood in the garden, his heart swelling for them. But his daughters would just giggle; his wife would look flustered . . . And Arif? He no longer knew what Arif would do. He only knew that he himself would feel foolish.

On the Saturday he went into the stock-room of the Empire Stores and fetched some choice items: chocolate fancies, iced Kunzle cakes. There was little demand from his customers for these high-class items. Only the best would do, however, for those who lived in Potters Bar.

It was a cool, blustery evening. There must be a storm blowing up. Kentucky boxes bowled along the pavement. Further up the street a man stood in a doorway, bellowing. It was an eerie sound, scarcely human. Hamid buttoned up his jacket as he left the shop, carrying his parcels. Far down the street he heard the smash of glass: he clutched the parcels to his chest.

Then it happened. He was just getting into the car. As he did so, he chanced to glance back across the street, towards the parade of shops. It was at that moment that

the door of the sauna and massage opened and Arif stepped out.

Within him, Hamid's heart shifted like a rock. He could
not move. The face was in shadow; all he could see was
the glow of a cigarette. Arif smoking? For some reason
this only faintly surprised Hamid.

There the boy stood, a slight figure in that familiar blue
and white anorak. He turned to look back at the door;
then he turned round and made his way across the road,
towards Hamid.

Hamid stood. He opened his mouth to cry out, but
nothing happened. Then, as Arif neared him, the street-
light fell upon his face.

It was a thinner face; thin, and knowing, and much older
than Arif. An unknown, shifty, Englishman's face.

Hamid climbed into his car and fumbled with the key.
His hands felt damp and boneless. He told himself to stop
being ridiculous; he felt a curious sinking, yet swelling
sensation, as if he had aged ten years in the last moments.

Driving home, he tried to shake off his unease. After all,
it had been a stranger. Nothing to do with his own cher-
ished son. Why then could he not concentrate on the road
ahead? He was a level-headed fellow; he always had been.

Sharine was in a state. 'Where have you been?' she cried.

'It's only ten o'clock,' he said, and asked, alarmed:
'What's happened?'

'What's happened? I've spilt the dahl and dropped the
sugar and, oh my nerves.'

She was standing in the kitchen. The air was aromatic
with cooking.

'The children have been helping?'

'The girls, yes, until I sent them to bed.'

'Arif?'

She shrugged. 'Him, help me?'

'Where is he?'

'Where he always is.'

Hamid walked up the stairs, up past the first landing, then up the narrow flight of stairs to the attic. For some reason he needed to see his son. He knew he would be there, but he needed to see him.

His heart thumped; it must be those stairs, he was no longer as young as he was. Thud, thud, went Arif's music. Hamid knocked on the door.

'What is it?' Arif's voice was sharp, yet muffled.

'It's your father.'

'Wait.'

A few sounds, then Arif opened the door.

'What do you do in there all evening?' asked Hamid. 'Why don't you help your mother? We have a tea party tomorrow.'

Arif shrugged.

'Why don't you answer my questions?' asked Hamid. 'Why?'

A pause. Arif stood behind the half-open door. Outside, the wind rattled against the slates. Finally he said: 'Why are you so interested?'

Hamid stared. 'And what sort of answer is that?'

'Ask yourself.' Arif slowly scratched the spot on his chin. 'If you have the inclination.'

And he slowly closed the door.

That night there was a storm. The window panes clattered and shook; the very house, his fortress, seemed to shudder. In the morning Hamid found that out in the garden some of the balustrade had fallen down. It was made of the most crumbly concrete.

'Charming,' said Mrs Yates. 'Love the wallpaper, awfully daring. And what sweet little girls.'

Tea cups clinked. Sharine, in her silk sari, moved from one guest to another. Her daughters followed her with plates of cakes. Everything was going like clockwork.

174

Looking at the pleasant faces, Hamid felt a flush of satisfaction. It had all been worth it. The years . . . The work . . .

'And where's the lad?' Mr Thompson asked, jovially.

'He'll be down,' said Hamid, looking at the door and then at his watch. 'Any minute.' Silently, he urged Arif to hurry up.

Mr Thompson's wife, whose name Hamid unfortunately had not caught, finished her cup of tea and said: 'Would it be frightfully rude if I asked to see the house?'

Mr Thompson laughed. 'Rosemary, you're incorrigible.'

Other guests stood up, too: Mr and Mrs Yates from next door, old Colonel Tindall from down the road, the teenage girls belonging to the widowed lady opposite.

'A guided tour,' joked Hamid, gathering his scattered wits. 'Tickets please.'

Sharine stood in the middle of the lounge, holding the tea pot. She looked alarmed but he gave her a small, reassuring nod. After all, the house was spick and span.

He led the way. Upstairs he pointed out the view from the master bedroom; the bathroom en suite.

'Carpets everywhere!' said Mrs Yates. 'And what an original colour!'

'Must have cost you,' said Mr Thompson, man to man. Hamid nodded modestly, his face hot with pleasure.

'What's up there?' asked Mrs Yates.

'Just the attic,' said Hamid.

But before he could continue, she had mounted the stairs and Mrs Thompson was following her.

'Rosemary!' called Mr Thompson, and turned to Hamid. 'Women!'

Hamid hurried up the stairs. Thud, thud . . . the narrow treads shook, he could hear above him the thump of Arif's music, and then he had arrived at the landing and one of the women was pushing open Arif's door.

'May I?' she turned and asked Hamid.

But by then she had opened the door.

There are some sights that a person never forgets. Sometimes they rise up again in dreams; in his sleep Hamid saw mottled faces, their skin bleeding, pressed up against the glass of his shop. He saw stumps raised, waving in his face, in those long-forgotten alleys in Lahore. All the wreckage of this world, from which he had tried, so very hard, to protect those he loved.

Through his life, which was a long and prosperous one, he never forgot the sight that met his eyes that Sunday afternoon. Arif, sprawled on the bed, his eyes closed. Arif, his own son, snoring as the men snored who lay on the pavements. On the floor lay empty cans of lager and two scattered magazines, their pages open: *Mayfair* and *Penthouse*.

Explosions, riots and wreckage all around the turning world. The small hiss of indrawn breath from the two women who stood beside him.

Stiff Competition

I knew I shouldn't have gone to the Fathers' Class. Well, would you? Perhaps you're the pseudy participating type. Perhaps you're one of those gonad-less *Guardian* readers who talks about growing with your wife. There's plenty moved in round our way; they never close their blinds so you can see what sharing lives they're leading, him at the sink, her working on her gender grievances. There's always those corduroy sag-bags on the floor, where they talk things through.

I don't. When they're exposed to the frank air, all those little mysteries wither away, don't they? Well, in this class we'd learn how to breathe them through. Breathe her, the wife, through childbirth, that is. Angie said it was all about facing one's emotions. I'd faced mine; they told me I didn't want to go. But I wasn't allowed to face that particular one. Illogical eh?

We'd all have to lie down on cushions; that's what she said. I'd feel a right berk.

But I had to go. She didn't tell me to, of course. She just exerted that familiar old pressure, like a thin iron band slowly tightening round my skull. We've had it about my smoking and the way it's always her who phones her parents (well they're her parents aren't they?), and the way she always has to phone mine (well?). And how I hadn't opened the Mothercare catalogue she'd left on my desk. It's got worse since she's been expecting.

So we went. We were going to go up in the lift but it

179

said MAXIMUM 8 PERSONS and there were already eight women in it, all massively pregnant.

'Tut tut,' I told them, pointing to the sign. 'Tut tut, ladies.'

Their heads turned slowly, like a herd of cows. They didn't get it.

As we climbed the stairs Angie sighed. 'I wish you wouldn't get facetious,' she said. 'Just because you're nervous.'

'I wasn't facetious. Just accurate.'

She was starting to pant. 'You find it a threat, don't you,' she puffed. 'This sort of thing.'

I didn't answer because by now I was puffed too. Must be all those fags.

Upstairs Angie disappeared on her hundredth daily visit to the loo. I went into the room. There were rows of chairs facing a screen, and a giant, unpleasant-looking plastic object on a plinth. Amongst the vast women sat their small men; they wore that smug look people have when doing their duty, you see it on drivers when they pull in to let a fire-engine pass, or voters emerging from a polling-booth. What a load of wets. I'd seen a promising-looking pub opposite the hospital. I wondered how many of these blokes wished they were sitting there with a pint of Fullers in front of them. I wondered how many of them admitted it.

I sat down next to an inoffensive, bespectacled chap.

'Sorry,' he said. 'This seat's taken.'

I sat one seat further away. There was something familiar about that voice. I looked at him again.

'Bugger me,' I said. 'It's Condom.'

He stared at me. Then he said: 'Nobody's called me that for fifteen years.'

'Who'm I then?'

His eyes narrowed. 'You look awfully familiar . . .'

'Go on. Guess.'

180

It took him ages. Finally he said slowly: 'It's not . . . Slatterly?'

I nodded.

'Sorry,' he said. 'I didn't recognize you.'

'You're looking at my gut? Married, aren't I? That's a Married gut.'

There was one of those pauses. What the hell could we say?

So, I volunteered. 'Here we are then, back in school.'

He paused, and his Adam's apple moved up and down: 'Older, wiser, but still with a lot to learn.'

What a prig! He'd always been one, of course. Edward Codron . . . Condom. His nickname had been laughably unsuitable. Once we'd been in the cloakroom, four of us, engaged in what we called Stiff Competition. I won't go into details but the general gist was that first one to fill a matchbox won. Anyway, creepy Condom came in and would you believe he reported us to the Head? You didn't do that sort of thing.

Still, he and I had been kind of friends – not mates, friends – because we lived in the same street. Anglepoise Mansions, I called his house, both his parents being professors.

'Lots to catch up on,' I said. 'Bet you went to university.'

He nodded. 'Jesus.'

'Pardon?'

'Jesus, Cambridge. And you?'

I shook my head. 'Insurance.'

He wore a cord jacket, Hush Puppies and a badge saying PROTEST AND SURVIVE.

I said: 'Bet you teach in a poly.'

'How did you guess?'

'I can tell.' Another pause. Then I said: 'One thing I needn't ask you . . .' I gestured at the other couples. 'If you got married.'

181

He coughed. I remembered his little cough. 'Actually we're not. We're living together.'

Now what the hell can you reply to that? I glared at him. Weedy old Condom, eh? By A-levels he was the only one in the history group who hadn't got his leg over. Well, who'd admitted it. After all, Bayliss used to frequently show us a different pack-of-threes, but I'd always suspected he'd just rotated them. Devious bastard. He ended up a barrister.

The hall was filling. I gazed furtively at Condom. He'd not only impregnated, but illegally. There's something irritatingly highly sexed, isn't there, about unmarried couples. Compared to married ones.

As if on cue, Angie came in. She sat down, lowering her weight with a sigh.

'Meet the wife,' I said.

'I have a name.'

'This is Angie,' I said. 'And this is Condom.'

'Edward Codron.' He leaned over to shake her hand.

They had one of those conversations about where are you living now? Condom, thank God, lived miles from us. How was he going to introduce his what's-her-name, when she arrived? If he didn't, how would I? Lover? Partner? Life-Comrade? I resented him having to make me decide, just because he wanted to make some social bloody statement.

Come to think of it, he'd always done things thoroughly; doggedly carrying them through. He'd been a terrible swot. Nobody admitted they crammed for exams, except him. He didn't even drink. And there was I, numbed with hangover in assembly, 'Oh Come, Emmanuel' hitting my head like a gong. The wickedest thing he played was chess. I thought: bet he drives one of those neutered little Citroëns, putter-putter, that I'm always getting stuck behind.

'What was he like at school?' asked Angie, indicating me.

'Terry? He wore winklepickers. He was a real tearaway.'

'No!' Angie gazed at me.

'Don't look so surprised,' I said.

'He smoked Players Untipped,' said Condom. 'Quite a Jack the Lad.'

'Really?'

Her look annoyed me. I said: 'I went out with the birds from the art school. Twiggy eyelashes . . . thick white lipstick . . . long thighs . . .'

'I painted on my lashes with charcoal,' said Angie. 'I remember now.'

'You didn't.'

'You didn't know me then,' she said. 'You don't know what I was like. You've never asked.'

'Course I have.'

'You haven't.' She paused, then smiled. 'And just look at us now.'

'This is what you did it for,' I said.

'What?' asked Condom.

'This,' I said, gesturing round. 'Reproduction.'

Then a woman came into the room. She was a gigantic creature in one of those Indian tents that liberated, fat women wear. She started to chat to us, and introduced the plastic thing which she called, with a simper, Pauline the Pelvis. Everyone sat in solemn silence. I remembered our Biology classes, fifteen years before . . . The raucous giggles, our teacher stuttering. But we were older now; we'd put our matchboxes behind us. Today nobody laughed.

In fact Angie was holding my hand – there, in front of everybody. She had called this an important moment for us both. I watched Pauline the Pelvis being tilted back and forward and thought of all the pelvises, or pelvi, I must have known, unbeknownst to me.

By now the tent was burbling on about relationships, and how the birth process was about bonding, and opening up to each other. I thought: they've opened. I pictured, with longing, a pint. A bag of dry-roasted peanuts. Nobody talks about relationships in pubs.

'Your hand's clammy,' Angie whispered.

'S'not mine, it's yours.'

'Terry, don't be tense.'

It was then that they opened the cupboards and started taking out the cushions.

'They're not for us as well?' I hissed. 'The blokes?'

'Of course. That's the point.'

'Can't we just watch?'

It was at that moment, when my mouth had opened for the next sentence, that the door opened and Sue walked in.

I froze; it was her. It was Sue. Her blonde hair was curly now; her smock billowed in the breeze from the fan and she was walking straight towards me.

'Ouch!' whispered Angie. 'You're hurting.'

I let go her hand. Sue came nearer.

'Darling,' she whispered to Condom, 'have I missed a lot?'

Her face looked scrubbed; her skin bleached and freckly. Those light-blue eyes . . . She looked cleaner, and older, and even more beautiful.

She sat down beside me, hip to hip. You know the saying: his bowels turned to water? Mine felt like that. At any moment she would recognize me. She mustn't.

Sue, of all girls. *Sue.* I kept my face turned away.

I was gazing straight into Angie's eyes. 'What's the matter?' she whispered.

'Nothing.'

'We'll all be doing it together. You needn't be worried.'

'Me, worried?'

Chairs scraped as everybody stood up. I tried to escape but Condom tapped my shoulder. 'This is Susan,' he said.

She said 'Hello' before she met my eye. Then she said: 'Good grief.'

Condom said: 'You knew each other?'

She paused. 'Briefly. Slightly.'

'Terry was just talking about girls from the art school.' He turned to her. 'But you've never mentioned him.'

She smiled. 'We hardly knew each other.'

My shirt was sticking to my armpits. Now we were all walking over to the cushions. I tried to nudge Angie towards the far corner but Sue and Condom were behind us, and when we were told to lie down we all lay down together. Angie on one side of me; Sue the other.

The Indian tent picked its way amongst us, smiling down. 'First we have to relax. I know this may seem strange to some of you ... We'll be doing First-Stage breathing ... Deep breaths, one, two, three ...'

In the corner of my eye I could see the dome of Sue's belly. Stretched out beside me, she was breathing heavily, in and out, as instructed. I could smell her perfume.

Sue and me, lying beside the gas fire. I'd got the living, breathing Sue in my arms. Her suede mini-skirt up around her waist ... her leg wrapped around me ... and my hand sliding down through the elastic waistband of her tights ... we were rolling over, bumping against the fender ...

'OK? Relaxed? She's fully dilated by now, and moving into the Second Stage of labour ... Time for the shallow pants.'

Sue, panting in my ear ... the rasp of her tights as she rearranged her limbs ... she'd done this before. After all, she was an art-school girl ...

'Can I?' *My voice was husky; I had to clear my throat.* 'Can I?'

I squeezed my eyes tight shut. Around me, rising and falling, they were panting *en masse*.

'Can I?'

'Yes.'

But could I?

'The contractions are coming on stronger now, keep panting, with each wave . . . Each wave growing more and more powerful . . .'

Crouched over myself, I was lumbering to my feet to switch off the light . . . behind me she lay waiting, glowing in the firelight . . . I was fumbling for my wallet.

A whisper. 'Can I help?'

'Help by rubbing,' said the voice. 'Rubbing her back, Dads. Help by breathing with her, breathing her through . . . Now she needs your support . . .'

Crouched there, my trousers round my ankles. I kept my back to her. Silence. I could hear her breathing behind me, waiting.

Stealthy, crackling sounds. My hands big and useless as sausages. And there it lay, dwindled . . .

I sat, hunched like a miser over my humiliating little offering.

'She's needing reassurance now, Dads. The contractions are much, much stronger . . .'

'You all right?' she asked.

Untruthfully, I nodded.

She put her arms around me. 'You've done this before?'

A pause. Then, untruthfully, I nodded again.

She set to work, tender and deft. Tenderly she tried, with her warm hands.

No bloody good.

All those matchboxes . . . all those sessions in our Arctic toilet . . . and in my creaking bed, through the wall the answering scrape-scrape of my sister's hamster going round its wheel. And when it came to it . . .

'Terry.'

A hand touched my arm. I jerked upright. Angie was sitting up, so were the others. I heard grunts as the women got to their feet.

Angie dusted down my suit, and smiled. 'You did it

marvellously. Sounded as if *you* were having the baby, not me.' She paused. 'Wasn't so bad, was it?'

Behind my head I heard Sue murmuring to Condom. Was she telling him about it now? Or would she save it till later, for the togetherness time on their corduroy sagbags? Some things are best left unsaid . . . But you can bet they'd talk *this* through.

Laugh it through, more like.

'It's the film now,' Angie said. *'Tamsin is Born.'* She paused: 'Where are you going?'

'I'll wait in the pub.'

She pulled me back. 'Terry, don't feel threatened. I've seen it before, it's terrifically moving.'

'Well, I'm moving terrifically fast.'

'Darling – look, it's no reflection on your masculinity or anything if you find it a bit overwhelming. Nobody will mind.'

'I'll faint,' I said. 'I'm off.'

But just then the lights were extinguished and it was too late. Grey numbers wobbled on the screen and I was trapped. The film began, in startling technicolor.

And when tiny, red Tamsin was born, shall I tell you what happened?

Condom passed out. He did, no kidding. There was this scrape, as his chair tipped over.

Later, in the pub, I said: 'Fancy old Condom fainting.'

Angie gazed at me over her orange juice. 'You're smiling.'

'I'm not.'

'Why? Why this macho power-game, this stupid competitiveness? What are you afraid of?'

I shrugged genially. I was well into my second pint, Jesus, it tasted good. I lit my third fag. I felt better. She couldn't get at me now.

Then she spoilt it. She sighed and said: 'Your nice friend, what's-his-name?'

'Condom.'

'Edward. He doesn't behave like that.' She gazed at me. Around my skull the band tightened.

'Behave like what?'

'Behave as if he's frightened of failing.' She paused, then she said: 'Real men don't.'

Buzz

An Eighties Soap Opera in Five Parts

EPISODE ONE: *In which our Heroine
gets Clamped, Tosses a Salad
and Makes a Decision*

It was an October evening and Buzz sauntered through the perfectly-formed streets of Covent Garden. Around her rose the most desirable commercial and residential units in London – witty conversions, stratospherically-appreciating penthouses, post-modern offices still busy with late-night achievers. If she closed her eyes she could hear, like faintly-rustling corn, the swift rise of property prices.

What a brillo place to live, and wasn't she lucky to have moved here just in time! A few years ago, when she first came to London, these streets had still been scruffy, what with the fruit market, and drunks, and squatters growing lentils in their window-boxes. Now that scene had gone, and it had been styled up to become the most fashionable area in London.

What she liked was the way that everything had been converted into something else. What once had been an old vegetable depository had become the B-Scene Gourmet Video Diner, where celebrities ate coulis of Tuscan dandelions and, surrounded by fractured mirrors and banked consoles, watched themselves appearing in old B movies. What had once been an old surgical appliance warehouse had become Trusses, *the* place for designer bondage. Then there was the corner pub. Once it had been The Jolly Carpenter, full of darts fixtures and unreconstructed old men. Now it was restyled as Sneers, the restaurant where you had to practically answer an examination paper on your own appearance to get in. At lunch there she could go table-hopping, her second-favourite activity.

191

She was giving up her first, now that Boris had moved out of her flat and her life. From now on she was going to succumb to the magazine articles and devote herself to the New Celibacy. Tonight, to celebrate her first meal alone, she was going to make herself a cleansing salad. A mile away there was the only late-night supermarket in London that sold Extra Virgin Raspberry Vinegar.

She was going to catch up on all those videos she'd taped but never had time to watch; she'd put on that new kumquat face-pack she'd never dared wear when Boris was around. She'd tell herself she didn't miss him, or his half of the incredibly expensive mortgage. Bugger Boris. In fact, knowing his busy gender-hopping schedule, somebody probably was, right now. Like all her men, Boris had been Bad News. They'd all been too old, too married, too sadistic, too gay. And he hadn't really loved her; in their nine months together he'd never even bothered to get a Residents Parking Permit for his Merc.

She climbed into her Golf, started the engine and drove to the supermarket.

It was one October evening, in a late-night supermarket, that Bernard's life changed. Or at least his lifestyle did, and that can come to pretty much the same thing.

He was feeling low. For a start, he'd just lost his job, teaching at the Inner London Evening Institute. They had cut his course, which was called 'Fun with Your Tropical Fish', and replaced it with 'An Introduction to Your Investments'. People weren't into fun anymore, it seemed; in this autumn of 1987 they were into money.

For another thing, he couldn't decide between a Vesta Curry-For-One or a Toad-In-The-Hole TV Dinner. He gazed into the deep freeze. The 'For One' sunk him further into gloom. Outside he heard the hooting of taxis and the tapping heels of women he would never meet. London seemed large and harsh and hostile, and harmless hobbies had been officially removed from the rates.

To make matters worse, his wife had left him and his house was up for sale. Soon he would be homeless. Where could he go, he and his collection of old Beatles records and his back numbers of *Which?*, in this city of rising house prices and shrinking romance? He thought bitterly of his ex, Audrey. If only they'd had a *Which?* issue devoted to wives. He would have chosen one with a more reliable performance and a longer guarantee.

There was only one other customer in the supermarket, a terrific-looking girl of about twenty-five. Red hair, creamy skin. Like everybody of her age, she was dressed in black – short black skirt, black tights, clompy black shoes. London nowadays reminded him of a holiday he'd once had in Greece – all the women dressed in black and looking at him as if he came from another country. Was thirty-five so terribly old? He couldn't help it if he could remember where he was when Kennedy was shot – at home, actually, inking his initials on his tennis balls; he'd led a quiet life.

He felt like saying something witty to her, like 'hello', but then he noticed she had a Walkman on so she couldn't hear anything anyway. This made him feel even more depressed.

He decided on a Fray Bentos Steak-and-Kidney Pudding. Just for a change.

Buzz was coming out of the supermarket when she heard a faint bellow. She took off her headphones; Ry Cooder was left tinkling round her neck.

A man was standing on the pavement staring at something. 'Oh God!' he cried.

She followed his gaze and saw a small, battered car. It had been clamped. So had hers. The man turned to her, his face stricken.

'Is it your first time?' she asked kindly.

He nodded, and gazed at his car. 'I always thought clamp was something Japanese businessmen got on planes.'

She laughed. 'Follow me. I've had it done to me so many times I must be a clampogenarian by now.'

She looked at him: twinkly eyes, late thirties, gosh *old*, and terminally untrendy. Thinning hair, sports jacket and – her gaze travelled downwards – on his feet, how wonderful, a pair of *Hush Puppies*! The genuine article. They were cropping up nowadays in retro shops, of course, but you could tell with this guy that it was first time round.

So that's how they started talking. He introduced himself as Bernard Freeman and she said she was Buzz Networker. They walked the mile or so to the clamp office, to pay their fines. It was a warm evening, for October; the streets smelt of pizza and petrol fumes. She hoped they wouldn't bump into anyone she knew, but she could always pass him off as one of her clients.

He said he lived in Dollis Hill. She shrieked with laughter. 'Dollis Hill?'

'What's wrong with Dollis Hill?'

She stifled her giggles. 'Sorry. It sounds so deliciously suburban.'

She wished he'd ask where she lived, so she could reply 'Covent Garden'. She'd slip it in later.

They arrived at the clamp office. It was one of the better evenings; there was quite a crowd there. Queueing at the cash desk was almost as good as Langans, and marginally less expensive. First she spotted Zara Kitsch, the Polish dress designer, accompanied by an inebriated new toy boy. Then she spotted Henrietta Hyperbole, the whizzo book publicist, a bit of a Sloane but *wunderbar* at her job, which was helicoptering authors across the country and filling them with Bollinger.

'She specializes in the big blockbusters,' whispered

Buzz. 'You know, those novels that have one-word titles.'
She paused, and added admiringly: 'At present she's hand-
ling *Thighs*.'

Bernard sighed. 'Wish I was.'

'Not kidding,' said Buzz, misunderstanding. 'The
author's worth *megabucks*!'

So Buzz clamp-queue-hopped and Bernard smoked a
cigarette. He was trying to give it up but decided that
being clamped was in the High Stress bracket. By the time
he and Buzz had got back to their cars and were waiting
for the police to arrive they felt a certain bond between
them. Clamping brings people closer together.

They gazed at their two cars: his old, hers new. It was
way past his supper time and even the pubs were closing.
He wondered how he was going to find another job. He
told her he came into London once a week to teach an
evening class.

'What class?' she asked.

'This week it was going to be "Breeding Guppies".'

Buzz, who thought he had said 'yuppies', said with
surprise: 'You mean they need to learn? They seem to be
breeding all over the place.'

He shook his head. 'They're quite shy creatures really.'

'Shy?'

He nodded.

'Shy's not the word I'd use,' she said. 'Competitive, yes.
Upwardly mobile.'

Puzzled, he asked: 'You mean, swimming near the top?'

She nodded. 'Some people call me one, just because I've
got a Golf Convertible. Silly, aren't they?'

He looked at her, frowning. 'What?'

'You must know a lot about them,' she said, faintly
surprised, 'to teach something like that.'

'I've got some.'

'What?'

'About two hundred, actually,' he replied. 'I keep them in the lounge.'

'The lounge?'

'My wife used to complain. Three socking great aquariums of them.'

It was then that they realized there had been a misunderstanding, so that took a bit longer. By the time they had sorted it out, the clamp team had arrived and started unlocking their cars.

So that's how they came to have supper together. It seemed too late to do anything else. Buzz took him to her flat, which was at the top of a refurbished building near the Covent Garden Piazza. With the windows open, she said, you could hear tourists asking directions in twenty different languages.

Bernard, clutching his carrier bag, gazed at her decor. It all looked terrifically modern and uncomfortable. When he'd asked her what she did she'd said an environmental stylist but he hadn't a clue what that meant. It seemed to be something to do with property. He didn't recognize any of the magazines on her coffee table, either: *Blueprint, The Face.* He felt he had stepped into another world. Was this how girls lived nowadays? He remembered the old times, with his aquariums gently bubbling and his wife making origami out of old copies of *Woman's Own.* He obviously had a lot to learn.

Starting with salad. Say 'salad' and he thought of sliced beetroot and good old Heinz. But Buzz was bringing a lot of pinkish foliage out of her fridge. Frilly lettuces and things.

'The creep!' she cried. 'He's nicked my cress!'

The creep turned out to be her ex-boyfriend. The cress came from Barcelona and you could only buy it in one tiny little shop in Soho that was hardly ever open.

'Catalan cress,' she said. 'It's got a really high iron content.'

'You could always go out and suck some railings,' he suggested, but she didn't listen.

'He'll be back,' she said. 'I know it. I'll have to change the locks.'

The ex-boyfriend turned out to be somebody called Boris Malaprobe.

'Have you heard of him?' she asked.

Bernard shook his head. 'I haven't heard of anybody.'

'He used to be a shrink. I went to him, years ago, when I lost my Filofax. He ran a Bereavement Counselling Service – you know, when your life falls to pieces. I told myself I kept going there because he had Italian *Vogue* in his waiting room but soon I knew I was hooked. He's a very powerful person, and I'm a fool when it comes to older men.'

Bernard's spirits rose. 'Are you?'

'Filofax was a sideline. His main business was sex therapy – this was a few years ago, when people were still having sex, but the bottom fell out of the market.' She shook the lettuces under the tap. 'People aren't into each other any more, they're into their digestions. So he's become this incredibly successful diet doctor. He says there's more money in colons than cocks.' She started chopping up a carrot. 'He was a bastard. I've given up men.'

'That's a shame,' said Bernard gallantly.

'I used to be stupidly promiscuous. I read the *Observer* last Sunday and found I'd slept with four out of the six people in "Quotes of the Week".'

'Gosh.'

'A footballer, a newsreader, a rock musician and an MP.' She smiled nostalgically. 'He could only do it when I was wearing blue pyjamas.'

'He was a Conservative, then?'

'No. Labour.'

Bernard felt a bit shocked by all this. It was then that he remembered his contribution to the supper, and took his Fray Bentos Steak-and-Kidney Pudding out of the carrier bag. She gasped, as if he'd produced a dirty book.

'That's disgusting!' she said. 'Think of your cholesterol count.'

'I like steak-and-kidney pudding.'

'Remember Dickie Hart, who compered that game show, "Grin and Bare It"?'

He nodded. 'Where husbands and wives took off all their clothes?'

'Well, he had a dicky heart and it was here,' she pointed proudly to her bedroom, 'that he had his coronary.' She dropped the tin into the trash-can.

So they had pasta and salad instead. The pasta was blue. It was a special kind, she said, that you could only find in another tiny little shop in Soho that was nearly always closed. It looked as if it was made from old Italian peasants' trousers, and in fact tasted rather like it, but he didn't say anything. When she spoke about food she went all serious, as if going to these little shops was like going to church. Was she a yuppie or was she a foodie or both? He felt dizzy.

They drank two bottles of wine with supper. After all, they both had sorrows to drown – he had more but then he had ten years on her. He told her how he'd been a teacher at a small Catholic school, Our Lady of the Recession, but the school had been closed. He told her how he'd been a teacher at evening class but his course had been cut. He told her that his wife was divorcing him and taking most of his money. How hard-headed women seemed nowadays!

'You're a Seventies bloke, aren't you,' said Buzz.

Bernard shrugged.

'That was the Me Decade.' She drank. 'We're in the Eighties now, mate.'

'And what decade is this?'

'The Mine.' She drained her glass. 'My body, my money, my property.'

He paused, considering this. 'What property?' he said, at last, bitterly. 'I'll be homeless soon.'

There was a silence. Then Buzz said: 'I've got an idea.'

'What?'

'Come and live here.'

His lettuce leaf dropped from his fork. 'What?'

'You can help with the mortgage. You can keep Boris out. You look handy and I never have time to do things like that.' She inspected him. 'And you look quite safe.'

'Why?' he demanded, hurt.

'You drive a Morris Minor.'

'Thanks a lot.'

She smiled. 'And it'll be a lot more fun than Dollis Hill.'

So, next week, Bernard moved in.

Next month: Will Buzz regret her decision? Will Bernard learn to distinguish fettucine from linguine? And what's his ex-wife up to?

EPISODE TWO: *In which our Heroine gets Slapped, Plays with Mirrors and Pretends our Hero is Someone Else*

Bernard was cooking sausages again. Buzz's nostrils flared as she came into the kitchen and saw her flatmate, shovelling in Sugar Puffs with one hand and stirring a fry-up with the other.

'God help your arteries!' she cried, her mouth watering.

She opened the fridge. One day, perhaps, the *Sunday Times* might feature her in 'A Life in the Day'. In preparation for this she breakfasted simply on a thin slice of super-fibre toast. Bernard said it reminded him of when he was a baby and used to suck the doormat, but she ignored him. What did he know? Him and his Wonderloaf.

It wasn't just his eating habits that were cramping her style. There was all his stuff. He'd moved in a week ago and it was getting on her nerves. At a pinch, she'd decided, the tropical tanks could be passed off as amusing; besides, the luminous little fishes matched the lights on her video recorder. But the rest! Most of it was his ex-wife's stuff, from the house in Dollis Hill.

Audrey, his ex, had apparently run off with another woman. Bernard sloshed tomato ketchup (his buy) onto a sausage. 'She was OK for years,' he said. 'You know, sewing loose covers, keen on the garden. Then this leaflet came through the door. She thought it said *You and your Cystus*. That's a shrub. So she went along to this meeting, but it turned out to be all about cystitis. It had been sent from this women's centre and was very poorly roneoed.' He paused, munching. 'They all talked about how awful

200

men were, and how they gave you cystitis, and she fell in love with the leader. She's black, and called Bella Cose.'

'I read about her last week in *City Limits*!'

'So that was the end of our marriage.' He sighed, and mopped up his egg with a piece of fried bread. 'When I got jealous she called me sexist. When I got angry she called me racist. When I tried to keep the house she called me a capitalist. I couldn't win.'

'How pitifully seventies!' said Buzz. For some reason, the thought of Audrey Freeman irritated her. 'She's probably calling herself Audrey Freeperson now. Christ, social awareness went out with herpes. Break loose. Get rid of her stuff. Flog it at the Boot Sale this afternoon.'

Down in the Covent Garden Piazza it was all ready for the Boot Sale. The buskers and Scandinavian students had been cleared away. In their place were the serried cars of the local residents: Porsches, BMWs, those jeep things. From their boots spilled the fruits of heavy-duty consumer spending.

Bernard's neighbour was a chap with a pigtail who had forgotten to shave. He was muttering to himself as he took stuff out of his Audi: 'My executive toys . . . My bike with those tiny wheels, always felt a prat on that . . . My digital skipping rope that showed my hyperventilation rate, how embarrassing . . . oh dear, my wet-look bumfreezer from Camden Lock . . .'

It all looked jolly up-to-date, thought Bernard gloomily, as he opened his Morris Minor and arranged his wares. Nobody would want all these things that Audrey had bought with her Green Shield Stamps.

But soon people were crowding round and, to his amazement, he was deluged with customers. Girls pounced, squealing, on Audrey's crimplene minidresses and her boxed set of Perry Como LPs. Someone snapped up the hostess trolley; someone else grabbed the Tupperware digestive biscuit dispenser. 'It's genuine! I've read about this in *Arena*!'

Someone else turned to him. 'Are you a dealer? Where did you *get* this stuff?'

'It's mine, actually.'

The other car-boot sellers gazed wanly as Bernard's pile disappeared. When everything was cleaned out, a man pointed to his jacket.

'Early preppie, if I'm not mistaken,' he said. 'Adorable patches on the elbows! How about £20?'

So Bernard was left, shivering in the autumn air but flushed with success. He'd go and find Buzz, and treat her to supper – at his sort of place, mind you, where they served chips and a nice lot of them.

It was a bit cold, though. So he bought the wet-look jacket from the man next to him. It was black, with a red lining, and for the first time in his life he felt quite trendy.

Buzz was at Bellevue Wharf, putting the finishing touches to the Show Flat. Until last year this building had been a doss-house and the units were, well, compact. But that's where her flair as an environmental stylist came in. Take mirrors. With mirrors she could make a bathroom grow into a glittering space of narcissistic reflections, for the narcissistic high-flyers who would someday use it, to phone from the jacuzzi or to cleanse themselves, post-coitally, in the bidet.

She arranged a dummy bottle of champagne and two glasses. She'd come a long way from Luton, hadn't she? She blushed when she thought of her family. God forbid that they should ever turn up. They kept threatening to, but so far she had stalled them by saying she was too busy. She *was* too busy. She had become the sort of girl she read about in magazines. She had become the sort of girl who would live in a flat like this. It was funny to think that only a few years ago she had been a silly little teenager who had never heard of radiccio.

Just then the door opened and Bernard stood there.

She stared. 'Blimey!' she said. 'It's Engelbert Humperdinck!'

He touched his jacket, modestly. 'I bought it at the Boot Sale.'

She burst out giggling but he didn't seem to notice. He said: 'I've been trying to find this place for hours. Why's it called a wharf? It's miles from the river.'

'Everyone wants to live in a wharf nowadays.' She shrugged. 'Anyway, if you stand on the roof you could almost see the Thames, if they hadn't built all that stuff in between.'

'Like, half London?'

'We're not talking logic,' she said. 'We're talking status. Know how much these flats are selling for? We're talking *letterheads*.'

She showed him the living room: the Conran sofas, the tasteful prints, the Ansaphone set at 10, to flatteringly indicate the amount of messages the owner might expect. Upon these touches rested her success. In pride of place, lit like a shrine, stood the multi-stacked CD player and TV complex. The table was laid for a dinner party, and each day she squirted the flat with ratatouille fumes.

She indicated the kitchen. 'We're into gourmet security. We have 24-hour video cameras in the kitchen units.'

'Kitchen units?'

'Know how much a Bang and Olufson Pasta Centre is *worth*?'

Bernard started chortling. How could he chortle, in that jacket? Did he know what a wally he looked?

He walked to the window. It overlooked an interesting urban landscape: the Tesco car park, the Kwality-Discount Used Saree Emporium.

'Blimey,' he said. 'What a hideous view!'

She reddened. She wished he hadn't turned up. He was like some awful older brother who, just when she'd spent hours dressing up in her smartest clothes, told her that her hem had fallen down at the back. She must have been mad, to ask him to move in with her.

'It's not hideous, it's bustling and cosmopolitan,' she said. 'In case you haven't noticed, the East End is an up-and-coming area. It's very fashionable.'

'I expect they'll be installing bottle banks in Green, Clear and Appelation Controlée.' He gestured round. 'So what sort of mug's going to buy this place?'

'We have a four-point plan. One: we get a celebrity to buy one of the units. Two: we get a chum of mine, who hires out stretch limos, to leave one parked in the forecourt.'

'That socking great black thing I saw when I came in?'

She nodded. 'Three: I take a gossip-columnist out to lunch and sell them the story. Four: when the units start moving –'

'What, they're that flimsy?'

'Selling, moron. When they start selling, the celebrity has an option to return the flat. After all, the point of famous people is that they're never around.'

'That's disgusting!'

'That's property.'

He gazed at her, his eyebrows knitted. 'What's a girl like you doing in a job like this?'

'What's a guy like you doing in a jacket like that?'

Down in the foyer, builders were busy winching up what looked like a piece of church chancel over the door, and plastering it into place. Buzz pointed out a man, who was shouting instructions.

'That's Piers Ransacke-Smythe,' she whispered. 'An old Etonian, now big in architectural salvage.'

'Salvage?'

'He started by breaking up his old family home and sending it to the States. Now he buys up old churches, that people don't go to anymore, and flogs the features. You know, pulpits in penthouses, that sort of thing. You've no idea what a font will do for an executive washroom.'

Bernard gazed at her, scratching his head. 'So where do they put God, in the tannoy?'

She ignored this, and turned her back on him. He gazed out of the front door. Across the street wandered some dejected-looking old men, former residents of the doss-house. They sat on benches, drinking cider and staring into space. Nobody had salvaged them.

He turned to Buzz, to suggest that the old men could be re-installed as original features. She was talking, however, to a muscular Scotsman who was covered in plaster dust. They looked annoyingly intimate. The man slapped her on the rump. Bernard saw, with satisfaction, that this had left a large grey handprint on her leather trousers.

'Who was that?' he asked, when she rejoined him.

'The foreman, Robbie Glands. Fancies himself. In fact, he's my Ex-Rough-Trade.'

'You mean he isn't rough with you any more?'

'No, nitwit. I mean I've given up sex. I told you.'

Bernard gazed at her bitterly. Typical. Now that he was divorced, and shacked up with this nice-looking bird – willowy, red hair, that sort of thing – now that, at last, he was free for a legover situation, she pronounced it out of fashion. Just his luck. His sex life was obviously like his jacket – ten years out of date.

But in the end the jacket turned out to be his salvation. They were just leaving when a distant chanting could be heard, and round the corner appeared a ragged band of people holding up a banner. It said HOMES FOR PEOPLE!

'Oh-oh,' said Buzz. 'Here they are again. Homes for People! Who do they think are going to live here – gerbils?'

The protestors approached. At the front were two women. One was black and dungaree'd. The other seemed vaguely familiar. She had linked her arm with the black woman; she wore overalls and her hair was cropped short, but with a spasm of recognition Bernard realized he was staring at his own ex-wife, Audrey.

He grabbed Buzz's arm. 'Quick!' he said. 'She mustn't see me here!'

Buzz fished a pair of dark glasses out of her pocket. 'Put these on and follow me.' She led him to the stretch limo and opened the door. 'Get in!' she hissed. 'In that ghastly jacket they'll think you're a celebrity.'

Panting, Bernard slid into the back. Buzz got into the driving seat and they pulled out into the road, leaving the protestors behind.

'Will they really?' he called to her, across the acres of carpeting.

'Well, an old, sad sort of celebrity. Say, Neil Sedaka.'

Bernard hadn't the strength to protest. He sank back into the seat and took off his dark glasses, though it still stayed dark in the car because the windows were tinted. It had been a confusing day.

Next month: Will Bernard get his leg over? Will Buzz manage to change him? Will he manage to change her? And will she persuade him to give up white bread?

Buzz had fallen in love again. Disastrously, as per usual.

It all started, like a lot of things, at Sneers, her local restaurant in Covent Garden. Sneers was terrifically trendy, and it served the most obscure mineral water in London. Terry Terrine ran it. In the sixties he had been a cockney photographer, and had a *succès de scandale* by laying out women to look just like food. Then, like everybody else in the seventies, he'd got interested in eating, and began taking photos of food that looked just like women. Once, apparently, the Obscene Squad had confiscated his photo of a half-opened mussel and a couple of oranges. Now, in the eighties, food had become a full-time obsession; he'd turned restaurateur, and on his passport described his religion as 'Lunch'.

Buzz liked Sneers because the waiters were always asking her where she got her hair done. They were so chatty that it took ages to get anything to eat, but she didn't mind because it gave her more time to table-hop.

It was a whizzo place for this because the cunningly-placed mirrors meant that you could not only inspect yourself from every angle, and check that your hair gel was holding, but you could also see everybody else. The wall decorations, too, were brilliant. Terry had decided that stippling was passé, so he'd done nippling instead. This was a variation of what celebrities did in Hollywood, when they pressed their feet into concrete. Here, ambitious women had covered their breasts with emulsion and pressed them against the walls; it gave a clever, blobby

effect and you could spend whole lunchtimes guessing
who's were who's. *Une touche* vulgar, perhaps, but that
was part of Terry's barrow-boy charm.

That fateful day in December she was lunching with
Zara Kitsch, the Polish dress designer and a great chum.
When she arrived, Zara was marking down her last
month's orgasms in her Filofax – she had a detachable
page for this, you could only get it from Denmark. Zara
was one of the few people Buzz knew who still had a
vigorous sex life – everyone else was into serial monogamy
or old videos – but Zara was health-conscious and said it
decreased the chance of ovarian cysts.

They hardly spoke, though, because they soon spied
other chums and were off. In fact, the whole restaurant
was on the move, its clientele, like jack-in-the-boxes, popping up at one table and then another. Zara went over to
chat to Enid Tippex, the fierce fashion editor who could
Jaspar Conran anyone from obscurity to fame. Buzz went
over to another chum. He made pop videos, putting rock
musicians on to roof-tops with a lot of dry ice, or else
cramming them into diving suits and making them mouth
their songs, out of sync, at the bottom of Tufnell Park
Swimming Baths.

She went back for her radiccio starter and then, before
the radiccio main course, she table-hopped some more.
Sometimes she wondered what she'd do if Bernard, her
flatmate, should appear. He was so embarrassing. Gosh,
he even wore a corduroy jacket with leather buttons like
little footballs. She decided she'd have to pass him off as
some long-lost uncle, who just happened to have turned
up in London.

But luckily Bernard's appearance was unlikely, as he
still hadn't got a job, or any money, and would be staying
at the flat reading her old books. She shouldn't be thinking
of Bernard. It was much more fun here at Sneers, wasn't
it?

And then, when she got back to her table, there was this amazing bloke sitting there. He'd table-hopped his way right into Zara's empty seat. He had this sleeked-back hair, Mafioso-style, and he wore a creased white suit. The smoother the bloke, Buzz had discovered, the more crumpled his suit. His name was Axel and he made films – well, commercials, but that was an art form too.

So they started this amazing affair. She'd told Bernard she was through with men but Axel was so terminally tasty. He had a silver Ferrari with a built-in fax machine and cocaine pouch. He'd been just everywhere. The floor of his car was littered with parking tickets in eight languages. And apparently he was a bit of a legend. He'd put the last meadow in England that still had wild flowers in it under contract for shampoo ads; he'd bought a whole terrace of back-to-backs for a scones campaign. And once he'd flown an entire film crew, plus three models, to the Seychelles for a month, just to shoot underarms for a deodorant commercial. Maddeningly, he'd slept with all three of the models.

In short, he had style, and when you got down to it, that was the important thing. He even bought his bin liners from a little shop in Venice. He had a place in Soho, which was one notch better than Covent Garden, and as he sexually abused her under his leather duvet she closed her eyes and thought of all the famous names she'd seen in his filofax.

The trouble was, he was into pain. Hers. Why did she always pick men who despised her? He said he'd had an unhappy childhood, and that made him slap women about because he was trying to get back at his mother. But it still hurt when she sat down, and she spent a fortune on Pan-Stick so that Bernard wouldn't guess what had happened when she got back to the flat.

She never brought Axel home. She had this feeling, for some reason, that Bernard might not like him. Bernard was always making her feel uncomfortable; she wished he'd stop it.

'I'm making us bread-and-butter pudding,' said Bernard, when she got home one evening. 'You've been looking awfully peaky.'

'Actually, I'm going out tonight.'

He paused. He had a blob of custard on his chin, and his brown hair was messy, but his face was serious. 'Buzz . . .'

'What?'

'He's a creep.'

'You don't even know him!'

'I've seen what he's been doing to you. Does he knock you about because you're not well-enough designed for him?'

'Shut up!'

He gazed at her, frowning. 'Why do you go out with such lousy phoneys? Because you're such a lousy phoney yourself?'

She snorted, and made for her room.

'I'll tell him you're really called Alison!' he yelled. 'I'll tell him what you look like with your Nile Mud face-pack on!' She slammed her bedroom door shut. 'I tell him what you look like with that rubber thing on your head, when you're doing your highlights!' She heard him, yelling louder through the closed door. 'Why can't you be a nice, decent person and go out with a nice, decent person like me?'

She didn't hear the rest, because she blocked her ears with her hands.

And then, the next week, an amazing thing happened. Axel asked her to go away with him for Christmas. He'd told his wife (he was married, of course) that he was off on a shoot, and he'd booked a room in a terrifically discreet Cotswold hotel – wood fire, fourposter, the lot. What bliss!

Bernard was going to his sister in Hornchurch.

'Hornchurch!' she hooted.

'Who's talking? Who comes from blooming Luton?' He sighed. 'Now I'm a bachelor again they'll be giving me rude candles, and one of those pillows that says *Women On Top*.' He sighed again. 'I should be so lucky.' He looked at her. 'Why don't you stay here, Buzz, and we'll have Christmas together.'

'You know I can't.'

'Creeps like him don't believe in Christmas. They only believe in adultery.'

The trouble was – her parents. If she was embarrassed by Bernard, that was nothing compared to her Mum and Dad. Her Dad, Ted, worked for the Gas Board and her mother, Ivy, wore magenta cardigans and told everybody about Buzz's funny little ways when she was a baby. So far Buzz had kept them away, more or less, from her friends. However, when they heard she wasn't coming home for Christmas they announced they were coming up to London to do some Christmas shopping and to meet her new boyfriend.

Buzz confided in Bernard. 'What shall I do? If they see him, they'll – '

'Call the police?' He laughed, mirthlessly. 'In which case, they've got more taste than you.'

Suddenly, she had an idea. She put her hand on his arm. 'Bernard. Darling Bernard . . .'

Why had he let himself in for this? What was in it for him? Nothing, except Buzz's gratitude. He must be mad.

The doorbell rang. Buzz showed her parents into the flat. It was two days before Christmas and the place looked quite festive. Bernard had even unpacked his plastic church, dating from his married days, which lit up and played 'Good King Wenceslas'. Buzz had hooted at this but she was in no position to hoot. Not today.

'So you're the new boyfriend, Axel,' said her father, shaking Bernard's hand. 'Pleased to meet you.'

'Funny name, isn't it,' said Bernard amiably. 'Not many people are called after a car part.'

Buzz glared at him. They sipped their sherry.

'I must say, you're a big improvement on the other ones,' said Buzz's mother.

They sat down for dinner. Buzz looked tense, and only picked at her food. Bernard found himself warming to her parents, who seemed awfully nice. He wished he wasn't tricking them. It seemed such a rotten thing to do.

'I hope you'll look after our little girl,' said her father.

'I'm trying to,' he replied. 'With difficulty.'

'She usually has Christmas with us,' said her mother. 'But still . . . I'm glad she seems to be settling down. She used to have a knack of picking horrible men.'

'I know,' said Bernard. 'I've seen them.'

'Poncing about in their flashy cars,' said her father. 'Stuck up berks.'

'Dad!' said Buzz.

'I ask you!' he went on. 'One of them had a blooming pigtail!'

Bernard nodded. 'Right bunch of wallies. Never understood what she saw in them.'

'Shut up!' hissed Buzz, and added quickly: 'Darling.'

'Just because they knew how to pronounce things in restaurants,' he went on. 'Strikes me, she had her priorities all muddled up. In fact, I've been quite worried about her.'

He heard Buzz breathing heavily.

Her mother looked at them, her head tilted. 'You two going to get engaged?'

'I hope so,' said Bernard, looking at Buzz. She glared at him. 'We're very much in love.' He reached out to press her hand, but she snatched it away.

'I can see that,' said her mother, fondly. 'You make a lovely pair.'

'Have some more potatoes,' said Buzz.

'I'd love to marry her,' went on Bernard. 'But I don't think she wants to marry me. She doesn't think I'm trendy enough.'

'Axel darling,' said Buzz coldly. 'Why don't you tell them about your work?'

'Work?'

'Making commercials!' she hissed.

Flustered, Bernard said: 'Well, I've just done a cat food one.'

'Cat food?'

'There's this cat, and she's looking out of this window, and then it says "Things happen after a tin of Whiskas".' He stopped, and tried to gather his wits. 'I get around, you know. I've got a Ferrari. I've just been to Jamaica.'

'What was the advertisement for?' asked her father.

'Anoraks,' he said.

Her father stared. 'Anoraks?'

At this point the phone rang. Buzz disappeared. A few moments later she came back. She looked flushed.

'Er, that was an old schoolfriend,' she said. 'She's, er, just wants me to pop up the road for a moment. Bit of a crisis.'

Buzz rushed out of the front door. There was a pause. It was Axel – Bernard knew it. He'd escaped his wife for an hour, and Buzz was off for a quick tryst in Soho.

Suddenly, his blood boiled. Blast her. She'd tricked her parents, she'd tricked him, she was nothing but a cheap tart – a pseudy, posturing, hard-hearted little bitch. He'd show her.

Inspired, he turned to her parents. 'Look, I'd like to give Buzz a surprise. Why don't you two come down for Christmas dinner?' Grinning, he told them the address of the Cotswold hotel. 'Don't say anything, just come.' He glowered. 'After all, Christmas is the season of goodwill. And love.'

It was a horrible thing to do, and the next moment he regretted it. But who could blame him? It was Buzz's fault, and she deserved all she got.

Will Buzz ever talk to Bernard again? How's she going to get her own back?

Buzz runs into a
born-again lesbian and
plays a nasty trick

Buzz and Bernard were in a state of war. She had been seething ever since Christmas. For some warped reason Bernard seemed to have found the whole thing hilarious. Axel hadn't been seen for dust, of course, and this made Bernard even more smug. How could she stand him another moment? He sniggered at her phone conversations, he made fun of her friends, he polluted her kitchen with his vast fry-ups. How could she have any sort of life when he was around? He was nothing but a Seventies has-been – gosh, he could even remember when people grew avocados from pips.

All through January she plotted her revenge. Bernard was still looking for a girlfriend. He said if Buzz wouldn't have him thousands would but, gratifyingly, he wasn't having much luck. Nobody was into love anymore, he said, they were just into money, and he hadn't got any. Where had romance gone? he asked. He kept bullying her to introduce him to her girlfriends but no fear.

One night he went up on to the roof and there, in the moonlight, he saw their neighbour wandering around, reciting. 'Dreams of ecstasy,' he heard her murmur, and 'Midnight roses,' and then something about golden daffodils. He rushed downstairs, all excited.

'I've found her at last!' he cried. 'A woman with a soul. She's actually reciting poetry!'

'Not really,' said Buzz. 'She's working on a perfume account. She's probably speaking to New York on her portable phone.'

He'd gone all silent then, and serve him right. Despite his age, he was pitifully immature.

Inspiration struck at the end of the month. She was down in the City, working in an atrium. For years now she had been into glass. When she first came to London she had worked for a firm of estate agents, Chump, Fiddlestone and Slack. They were a dozy lot and she soon realized she could shift property quicker than they could, simply by using her imagination and a simmering casserole of *coq au vin*, which she carried from house to house and slipped into vendors' ovens before visitors arrived.

From there she went into conservatory building, because they'd become so fashionable that everyone wanted one, and the more elaborate the better. Sometimes, in fact, people couldn't pay for them at all and had to sell their house and move into the conservatory, camping amongst the aspidistras. You could recognize these families in the street because they were covered in greenfly. It was then she discovered that building an extension was like saying 'let's have another baby' – it meant a marriage was on the rocks and a couple would soon be splitting up anyway. So she'd sold off her conservatory concession to a firm of solicitors, who could save on overheads by doing the building and the divorce at the same time.

At this point she had moved into Covent Garden and become an environmental stylist. By this time conservatory fever had gripped the City, but now they called them atriums and an office wasn't an office unless it had a huge, galleried atrium that blinded passing planes. One firm of stockbrokers had apparently started a market garden in theirs, and now they made as much money from growing tomatoes as they did from insider dealing. Other firms started growing pinewoods, with the aid of Forestry Commission grants. They put up signs saying 'Keep to the Bridle Paths' because one organization had planted such a thick forest that they'd lost their vice-chairman for a week.

Buzz was working in an acre of tropical jungle. It filled the foyer of a merchant bank, down near London Bridge. Outside it was a frosty winter's day but around her the foliage gently steamed. She liked working here because it opened the pores and she could save on sauna bills. Through the foliage she could hear the cheerful whistling of a Brazilian Indian, who had been imported to tap the rubber plants. She liked him because he lent her his anklets.

That afternoon she was busy pruning when she heard a loud, female voice behind her. She turned. There stood a woman who said she was from some Black Minorities campaign.

'Do you realize this is exploitation?' the woman said, pointing to the Indian.

'But he's having a great time,' said Buzz. 'He's formed himself into a limited company called Ecosystems Maintenance, and he goes round offices tapping rubber and selling it to condom firms. It's an expanding market.'

'It's racist!'

'But he's loving it here. At night he goes to the Limelight, and *The Face* photographs him surrounded by pop stars' mistresses in leather bustiers.'

'Leather what?'

Buzz looked at the woman's boilersuit. 'Never mind.'

The woman shoved a piece of paper into Buzz's hand. There were so many campaigns on the letterhead that there was hardly room for anything underneath – *Wages for Lesbians Campaign, Campaign for Unwaged Lesbians Who Can't Find Their Way Out of the Barbican Centre*. Then Buzz looked at the name at the bottom, and dropped her secateurs. She was face to face, she realized, with Bernard's ex-wife Audrey.

She gazed at her, fascinated. Audrey was a beefy woman

with cropped hair. How amazing that once she had been a housewife with the biggest collection of freezer bags in Dollis Hill! How extraordinary, that once she had been married to Bernard! Nowadays she was a born-again gay and she lived with her co-person Bella Cose; they spent their time campaigning for things and being featured in *City Limits*.

Buzz suddenly had this brilliant idea. 'There's a man you must meet,' she smiled. 'When it comes to minority rights, you'll find him terribly supportive.'

'A blind date?' said Bernard, that evening. He paused, and looked at her suspiciously. 'Why are you being so kind to me, all of a sudden?'

'Let's just say I'm fed up with being so beastly.'

'A blind date, tonight?' He was just opening a steak-and-kidney TV dinner, but he put it back into the fridge. He frowned at her. 'She's a friend of yours?'

'A new friend.'

'Is she pretty?'

'Stunning. She stunned me.'

'But do you think we'll have anything in common?'

'Oh yes.' Buzz nodded. 'You'll have lots in common. I promise that.'

Stifling her giggles, she watched him waltz into the bathroom. She heard him splashing in the bath; she smelt her Body Shop Body Gel but for once she didn't mind. What divine revenge, to send him off on a date with his own ex-wife! They'd have lots to talk about; after all, he always said he was an endangered minority, being the only person in London who had never been to the Groucho Club.

Bernard disappeared in high spirits, and wearing his best suit. He was even missing his favourite TV programme, the Embassy Snooker Championships. She heard him down in the street, trying to start his car. Finally the engine coughed into life and he rattled away into the distance.

She was on tenterhooks all evening, picturing them. They were due to rendevous at Meet'N'Veg, a wholefood restaurant in the wrong end of Stoke Newington. She imagined their faces, when they saw each other. How soon before they started throwing tofu rissoles across the table? Bernard hadn't even realized that the place was vegetarian. She crawled under the duvet. How soon before he came home and started yelling at her?

She stuffed the duvet into her mouth. Minutes ticked by; her heart pounded. She knew it was silly; she should be out having a good time, not playing tricks on her flatmate. Think of all the tasty men she could be meeting and who would love to meet her. After all, she was the trendiest person she knew. She bought her knickers in Perugia; she bought her Mont Blanc pen refills from a little shop on the Lower East Side. Why was she wasting her energies on Bernard?

Midnight passed. She lay in bed, tense. What was happening? What on earth was he up to with his ex-wife – surely they must have finished their meal hours ago? Meet'N'Veg was one of those overlit pine places that closed depressingly early. Had they torn each other to bits by now? Audrey had been sending the most poisonous lawyer's letters these past three months. She obviously loathed Bernard – after all, he was not only her ex-husband but male, too – and she had been citing all the clothes she had washed for him over the years, sock by sock.

One o'clock passed, and then two. Down in the street she heard the voices of late-night revellers, clear in the frosty air. Drunken Scandinavian pop songs floated up to her window; she heard the familiar yelps of people who'd found their cars had been clamped. Faint filmtrack music came from the B-Scene Gourmet Video Diner.

She shivered. Her stupid heart was still pounding. Perhaps he had never got there; perhaps he had had an accident in his awful old Morris Minor. Perhaps Audrey had kicked him senseless with her Doc Martens and he was lying in the gutter of some drearily half-gentrified street in N something. Perhaps he was never going to come back at all.

In his bedroom she heard the soft bubbling of his tropical aquarium. She thought of his framed collection of beer mats; how she'd sneered at them! She thought of the night they had met, way back in October, when he had spoken to her outside the supermarket. It seemed ages ago; she actually liked Whitney Houston then, God, how embarrassing.

Her face felt hot and her eyes prickled. She shouldn't have sent him off like this; it was stupid to take revenge on him when he had really been right, all along. She *had* been pretentious; she *had* been a phoney. She had behaved so badly, and when he came home she would tell him so.

It was four o'clock, and down in the street the last cars were revving up. A solitary busker was making his way home; she heard the bleeps of his calculator as he converted dollars into sterling. Covent Garden was emptying; soon only its sleeping residents would be left. She realized, with surprise, that she didn't really know any of her neighbours at all; she just met them each morning when they were fighting for the single resident's parking space. She felt suddenly, ridiculously, lonely.

Five-thirty . . . six. At seven o'clock she finally got up and went into the kitchen to make some breakfast. She opened the breadbin. There, next to her high-fibre olive' n'cardamon bread sat his squashed packet of Wonderloaf. Her eyes filled with tears.

She was just putting on the kettle when she heard the front door open. She swung round.

Bernard stood there. His hair was messed up and there was blood on his cheek. She moved towards him.

Then she saw that it wasn't blood, it was lipstick. He had a strange expression on his face.

'Where have you been?' she asked.

He didn't reply; he hardly seemed to see her.

'What happened?' she demanded.

He looked – well, happy. He smiled dreamily, then he said: 'The most amazing thing's happened.'

'What?'

He paused. 'I've fallen in love.'

Next month: Who on earth has Bernard fallen in love with? Could it be Audrey? And what's Buzz going to do about it?

EPISODE FIVE: *Where Buzz fumes and Bernard blows up*

Buzz was seething. If only Bernard didn't look so damn smug all the time.

'Just because you're in love,' she said 'you needn't look so happy about it.'

'One day, creepo, you might fall in love.' He munched his meusli. 'Then you'll understand.'

That was another thing. For months she'd been nagging him about his disgusting eating habits – the oozing dough-nuts, the heart-stopping haze of cholesterol when he fried his sausages. Now, suddenly, along came this Emily crea-ture and here he was, a born-again fibre-phile. He was even starting to wear quite decent clothes. In fact, he could almost be seen in public. What had this Emily got that she hadn't?

'It's simple,' Bernard said. 'She's nice. She cares about me. She goes out with me.'

'She laughs at your ghastly jokes.'

He nodded. 'She doesn't mind that I've never eaten arigula.'

'I've only eaten it once!' She paused. 'Is she incredibly pretty?'

He nodded. 'Incredibly.'

He'd met this vision, apparently, at Meet'N'Veg, the wholefood restaurant. She'd come to his rescue when he'd found himself face-to-face with his ex-wife; when the fighting broke out she'd taken him back to her place. She was a nurse, in one of the few remaining hospitals that still had any, and she obviously ministered to his every

222

need, judging by his firmly-closed bedroom door, the two sets of breakfast dishes that appeared in the sink most mornings, and his generally revitalized demeanour.

'Why can't I meet her?'

'She's on the early shift. She leaves at six.' He paused. 'Anyway, you wouldn't get on. You're from a different planet.'

Buzz snorted, and went to work. Catch her trying to catch a glimpse of this amazing creature! Catch her being interested!

She was working on some conversions in Soho – tiny flats she was trying to enlarge with *trompe-l'œil* mural effects. They were being developed by Sir Monty Mortar, the millionaire builder and ex-porn king. Once he'd owned a chain of strip clubs and three vice rings. However, in the late eighties he had realized, like everyone else, that there was more money in property than in sex. As a result, he'd got a government grant to convert all his brothels into residential units. Only one remained, and this had been preserved as a tourist attraction. The National Truss had taken it over for the nation and installed, as custodian, a retired prostitute who sat at the entrance, wearing a twin-set and pearls. For a small donation she showed visitors around the peep-show room, carefully restored to its original chocolate brown, and the bedrooms, each complete with its antique red light bulb. There was also a small shop downstairs, which sold lavender-stuffed dildos and 'Spanking Schoolgirls' marmalade.

Buzz trudged along the Soho street. On each side it was lined with skips. They were filled with rubbish from the building works: date-expired condoms, deflated inflatable women, still pouting, and heaps of vibrators whose batteries were extracted by passers-by to put into their walkmen. She felt depressed. Sex was finished; nowadays everybody was into romance. Some of them had even got married and gone to live in the country. London didn't seem quite as brilliant as it once had been and for some reason her heart wasn't in her work anymore; she kept painting these naff cottage garden scenes – real choc box stuff – on the walls of the residential units.

She heard a burst of laughter from the Groucho Club but for once she didn't feel like going in. It had lost its charm. She felt like one of those deflated women – empty, and not wanted by anyone.

That night, when she was walking home, she glanced up at Bernard's bedroom window. She stopped. Emily stood there. She was tall, blonde and beautiful. She was motionless – obviously transfixed by Bernard's words of love.

Seething, Buzz went to bed.

The next morning Emily had disappeared but Bernard, who seemed in even better spirits than usual, said he had a plan for the three of them to get together.

'It's Valentine's Day on Sunday,' he said. 'Emily and I are having a special dinner, to celebrate our engagement.'

She stared. 'Engagement?'

'Why don't you come along, and make it a party?' He smiled. 'You've got to meet sometime.'

All that week she was in a turmoil. On Thursday she had lunch with her friend Zara Kitsch, and decided to confide in her.

'I feel terrible,' she said. 'I can't concentrate.' She pushed her sun-dried tomatoes around her plate. 'I'm not even into gourmet food anymore.'

'Darlink, you're so silly!' said Zara, in her charming Polish brogue. 'Don't you know your problem?'

'What?'

'You're in love!'

Buzz stared at her. 'I'm what?'

'I've known eet for months. Eet's written all over your face.'

Buzz paused. 'And who am I in love with?'

'With thees Bernard, of course. Really, Buzz. You theenk you're so street-smart, but in matters of the heart you're just a young girl from the suburbs.'

Buzz glared at her. 'So what of it? Much good it's going to do me. He's fallen for somebody else.'

On Friday she smudged a mural so badly that she had to paint it out and start all over again. Her hand trembled. Why had she been such an idiot all these months, not letting Bernard sleep with her? She'd been such a fool, taunting him with other men and never going out with him, in case anybody saw them. Actually, she'd grown rather fond of his tweed jacket with the buttons like little footballs.

That night she asked him: 'So when are you two going to get married?'

'As soon as poss,' he said. 'I'm already looking for a cottage in the country.'

'So that's where you've been all week.'

'You see, I've got a job in Sussex.'

'What job?'

'At a rehabilitation institute, teaching Rewarding Hobbies to bankrupt stockbrokers. Fish breeding, and things.'

'And what sort of cottage did you two have in mind?'

'Honeysuckle. Thatch. Dogs. Kids.' He paused. 'The normal sort of thing. You wouldn't be interested.'

'Bully for you.'

On Sunday she took two hours deciding what to wear. At six-thirty she tried to paint her nails but, humiliatingly, her hands were trembling. They were meeting at Sneers. Bernard had always sneered at Sneers, but she couldn't make him out nowadays. He had this twinkly look. He'd left early, humming happily and dressed in his best new suit. If only her hands would behave, she'd throttle him.

At seven-thirty she left the flat. Her stupid heart was pounding. It was a frosty night, and valentines were hung up in the windows of the 24-hour gift shops. I LOVE YOU winked one mockingly, in neon.

She hesitated outside Sneers. The place had been decorated with ribbons and candles; at every table there seemed to be a loving couple. She took a breath and stepped in.

She saw Bernard. He sat alone; probably Emily was in the Ladies, making herself even more beautiful. Buzz hesitated, and went over.

'Where is she?' she asked. Her voice sounded hoarse, as if she were being strangled.

'Who?'

'Emily, twit. Your fiancée. Who do you think?'

He pulled out a chair next to him. Buzz sat down. As she fiddled with her glass, she saw that the table was set for two. She thought she'd been invited for the whole meal, but it must be only for a drink.

Bernard cleared his throat. 'Buzz,' he said 'I've got something to tell you.' His voice sounded high and strained.

She looked at him. 'What is it?'

He paused. 'There isn't any Emily.'

There was a silence. She stared at him. 'What?'

'I made her up.'

Buzz felt her mouth falling open. 'But I saw her in your bedroom!'

'Oh, that. I found that in a skip, and blew it up.'

There was a long pause. The murmuring voices of the other people seemed miles away. Buzz didn't dare look up, in case she saw his face and realized he was joking.

He took a breath. 'That night, when you fixed up that meeting with Audrey – the fact was, I was so furious that I decided to pay you back.'

She lifted her head and gazed at him. Her heart pounded. 'Is that what you brought me here to tell me?'

He paused. Then he took her hand. 'Shall we call it quits?'

She nodded. 'OK. Quits.'

He smiled at her, his eyes twinkling. 'Would you, by any chance, consider a take-over bid?'

She smiled, and shook her head. 'No, darling. Let's make it a merger.'

THE END

Will Bernard and Buzz live happily ever after? Well, from now on it's up to them.